NEW SOUND

Books by Leslie Waller

Fiction

THREE DAY PASS

SHOW ME THE WAY

THE BED SHE MADE

PHOENIX ISLAND

THE BANKER

K

WILL THE REAL TOULOUSE-
LAUTREC PLEASE STAND UP?

OVERDRIVE

THE FAMILY

NEW SOUND

Books to Begin On

TIME

NUMBERS

WEATHER

OUR AMERICAN FLAG

OUR AMERICAN LANGUAGE

EXPLORERS

ELECTRICITY

AMERICAN INVENTIONS

THE AMERICAN WEST

CLOTHING

NEW SOUND

by Leslie Waller

PACESETTER

HOLT, RINEHART AND WINSTON
New York   Chicago   San Francisco

for Liz and Sue,
one more time

NEW SOUND

1

We arrived in two Rolls-Royces, baby. The screams hurt my ears.

I mean, like why not? The Beatles don't ride any cheaper wheels than Rollses.

So when Stacy Nova and the Flesh-Colored Band-aid arrive at a theater, man, it's in two Rolls-Royces. At least.

You might think, well, it's just me, Stacy, and three other cats. That's the whole group, me on piano and vocals, Eddie Getz on lead guitar, Mo Manzo on rhythm guitar and Georgie Whitefeather on drums.

So we could arrive in one Rolls, right? Wrong, daddy.

You have to know what this business is all about. Then you know why we rent two Rollses.

Oh, you thought we owned them? I guess that's what most of the cats and chicks think. I mean the ones standing around outside the theaters and the studios and the halls and the clubs and all the other places we work.

Well, we rent. We also rent an electric box for me on these crumby one-night stands. We also rent Georgie's bass drum and hi-sock cymbal.

Like, who needs traveling with all that hardware? The amplifiers are heavy enough. There's no room for a piano and all that.

Tonight we look great when we step out of those two Rollses. They're big long black mammas with real square stainless steel radiators. You'd think we owned every inch of them.

That's what this business is all about, man. You have to look like you owned the world.

When you step from the Rolls you hear the dolls screaming. They yell "Stacy! Stacy-Baby!" in that high, crazy way. Man, you know you own the whole world and everything in it.

This gig is in Chicago, my home town.

Sounds like the song, doesn't it? We do a groovy arrangement of it in half-time stop-time. You know, like the old-style soft-shoe dancers used to use? I work the number up front, without the piano. I give it enough pow to blow your mind in the last row of any theater.

Stacy Nova and the Flesh-Colored Bandaid always make it big in Chicago. I mean, Eddie Getz is from there, too. So that means half the group is down-homesville.

Anyway, we get out of these two big-mamma Rollses. The scream and the roar is enough to lift your wig clean off your scalp.

Man, it's beautiful. Get the picture?

These two giant heaps pull up to this TV studio building on the Near North Side. And this giant mob of teenies and screamies goes ape, right?

And the chauffeurs of the heaps hop out and open the rear doors. And out of the cars come these four cats in black leather jeans and ocelot jackets.

Georgie's is sleeveless so he can work the drums better. Mo Manzo wears this Navajo headband he picked up in Albuquerque. Eddie Getz wears three strands of bright blue beads.

Maybe you've been living under a rock. Maybe you don't know what I look like when I step out of the Rolls.

I'm the tall one of the four, right? And this year I gave up the Aussie hat with the brim turned up on the side. This year I wear a white silk turban. The biggest fake ruby you ever saw is in the middle of it, up front.

And, dig this, baby. Inside the turban is a little nickel-cadmium 1.5 volt storage battery. It has a little random-access switch I rigged up. And behind this big fat ruby are about six little bug-lights. You know the little, tiny baby kind?

And when I step out of the Rolls, daddy, those little baby bug-lights are flickering behind the ruby in

3

a random cycle. On. Off. On. Like a bunch of fireflies in the night.

So, like, man, you have to know it's me, Stacy Nova.

I mean, could it be anybody else?

2

🗋🗋🗋🗋🗋🗋🗋🗋🗋🗋🗋🗋🗋🗋

At the hotel this day in Chicago a girl reporter from the *Sun-Times* asked me how I felt about my "triumphal homecoming."

You dig? Triumphal homecoming, yet.

I said: "Baby, lay that on me twice?"

She wasn't bad. Older, you know, late twenties or so, nice smile. "I said, how do you feel about your triumphal homecoming to Chicago?"

The rest of the group had laid out of this interview. The chick was there with a photog. I was putting on a little act for the two of them.

You're hip to the scene, right? Like caviar and champagne for breakfast. Only breakfast is, like, one in the afternoon.

I mean, I wasn't always Stacy Nova. I didn't always get up in the p.m. It's no secret. The fan magazines print it enough times.

4

Back in the days when I was plain Stanley Novotny I lived on the West Side here in Chicago. I managed to wake up about like, say eight A.M. Because I had to be at school by quarter to nine, right?

So, naturally, I laid down a big put-on for this news chick and her photog.

"No, thanks," she said, when I offer her some of the fish eggs and bubbles. "I usually don't eat that well before sundown."

I think she meant to put me down, you know? But if there's one thing Stanley Novotny knows, it's how to handle a put-down. I knew how even when I was a kid of twelve. Now I'm almost twenty. There isn't anybody can put me down so I stay put.

"You don't dig plain, down-home cooking?" I asked the news chick. "If you don't have eyes for caviar and champagne at breakfast, how are you going to move up to high-class food for dinner?"

So she was smart enough to smile politely. I mean, she knew her put-down didn't work and wouldn't work. Not ever. So she copped out. I mean, like, she had the brains to see who she was up against.

That's something old people don't always have the brains to see. I mean, they figure age gives them edge.

Not ever. I've been putting down old people like this news chick since I was in junior high. You know what I mean. She wasn't really old. But she thought old, dig?

To show me she had brains, she came right back with one of those curve-ball pitches. "Is it true you don't trust anybody over thirty?" she asked.

Now, you know I never said anything like that. She got this jazz from somewhere else. It was some magazine article putting down young people for not trusting old people.

Me, I would never say anything like that. In this business, the public is under twenty and the artists are around twenty. But the guys who book the jobs, the guys who cut the records, the guys who spin the platters on the air, they are thirty or over.

So, baby, Uncle Stacy is hip. And no brainy news chick gets me to put down old folks in public.

Anyway, this day I'm talking about in Chicago, at the hotel, I decided to come on real strong. I wanted to rub this chick's nose in what a big man Stacy Nova was.

So, it wasn't long before the hotel manicurist, barber and shoeshine boy showed up. I mean, like, was this a scene.

The rest of the interview went on with me getting a trim, a manicure and a shine. I offered a manicure to the newspaper lady. She said no. I offered a shine to the photog. He said yes.

I offered caviar and champagne to the manicurist, the barber and the shoeshine boy. They said yes.

It was a great big happy group we had going. It

was eating the girl reporter's heart out. "Is this a typical breakfast scene for you?" she asked.

"No."

"You usually do without the retinue?"

I smiled. "This is no retinue, baby. These are just nice people."

"I mean—" She made a gesture with her hands as if to say "Stop bugging me."

"No, this is not a typical breakfast," I picked up. "Usually I have a masseur on deck, too." I rubbed my shoulder. "He lays mitts on me and works out the kinks."

"Do you have a lot of kinks?" she asked.

Now she was turning mean, see? "Not the kind you're familiar with," I snapped back. "Just muscle aches."

"Tension?" she asked.

"I told you, honey. It's not your kind of kink. This is from hard work."

She stared at me, real hard. I don't mean she was a hard chick. As a matter of fact she was kind of nice. But the look she gave me was a long one that said, "Boy, I am going to clobber you in print."

I said, "Sorry you don't like me, lady. I like you."

Her face went very bright red. "What makes you think I don't like you?"

I shrugged. "Just that giant, economy-size chip on your shoulder."

"I don't have to like everyone I interview."

"I don't have to like everyone who interviews me," I said. "But I like you."

"I'm charmed," she said. "Is that what I'm supposed to be?"

I made a now-you-really-hurt-me face. "Is that nice?"

She busted out laughing. I'm pretty good at the face-making bit. Now we were friends. So I let up on the pressure.

"You from Chicago, too?" I asked.

She nodded and told me what high school she went to. I told her the name of my high school. We were off and running nicely.

You see, you have to know how to handle old people.

3

I guess I've been handling old people most of my life. Why is it you can't grow up in peace, unless you've fought and conned your way past a whole army of old people?

I don't think about it too much. It just gets you

bitter to think about it. When you're bitter, it starts to show in your performing.

Probably it was thinking about that time in Chicago that started me off. That whole day-and-a-half in Chicago happened—when was it—eight-nine months ago?

I can still remember the whole thing. It's very clear. Out of all the one-night stands the Flesh-Colored Bandaid plays, I can't recall even a half-dozen.

But I remember that gig in Chicago. I suppose it's because we did so great there. I mean we killed 'em.

Maybe it was the idea of getting back home, too. Maybe it was the way the crowd loved us. Maybe it was putting on the girl reporter. Or reading the whole story the next morning in the *Sun-Times*.

Or maybe it was knowing that they were reading it, too.

The old folks. My mother and father.

That's right, baby. I split the Chicago scene maybe a year before, blew school and hit the road. And the first time they heard from me was that morning when they read the *Sun-Times*.

I know. Eddie Getz says I'm too cool to be real. I mean, to each his own bag, right? Eddie writes his folks once a week. That time we played Chicago, he phoned them. He stayed overnight with them.

Okay, that's his thing. They dig each other. But, baby, it sure isn't my thing.

9

Every paper in town wanted to interview us. Home-town boys make it big, you know. But the only one I'd okay for an interview was the *Sun-Times* because it's the one my folks read.

The funny thing is, I went to all that trouble for nothing. Because to this day I don't know if they really read the story. They didn't let me know it. And, of course, I wouldn't be about to ask them.

I mean, all lines are down, dig? I can imagine the whole bit at the breakfast table.

"Good God," my old lady would say. "Charley, will you look at this?"

My mother thinks I resemble him. But where I'm tall, he's broad and where I'm dark, he's sandy and where I try to stay with it and dig the scene, he's dropped out of life a million years ago.

That's my old man.

If you were just meeting him, you wouldn't have any idea why I feel the way I do about him. On the outside he looks like everybody else. I mean, he makes a career of it.

In this day and age, he doesn't own any kind of shirt but white. He's got these black, round-toed shoes that look like he bought them at a Navy surplus store. I mean, he's got two pair and they look exactly the same.

He has these spectacles with frames that are half plastic and half gold. He parts his hair on the side.

He keeps it real short, especially over the ears and in back.

There is always a pencil or a pen sticking up slightly from the breast pocket of his jacket.

He wears a hat all year. He takes off his hat in elevators if a woman gets in. He tips his hat to women he knows on the street.

Oh, I forgot the bulges. He's a little overweight, naturally. So his clothes are a little tight all the time. I mean, the button on the front of his suit jacket is always about to tear loose.

But he carries things in his pockets. I still know what all of them are.

There's the bulge in his right rear pocket. That's his key folder with about ten keys to different locked things. There's a bulge in his left rear pocket. That's a spare handkerchief.

There's a bulge of loose change, quarters, nickels and such in his right hip pocket. The opposite bulge is a roll of one- and five-dollar bills.

The bulge in the right-hand pocket of his coat is a pouch of tobacco, a pipe, a little box of wooden matches and a three-part thingie to clean out the pipe and all that.

The bulge on the other side is a grooming kit. I am leveling, baby. A comb, a nail clipper, a nail file and a brush kind of thing for flicking off lint. Oh, and another handkerchief.

The bulge in the inside right-hand pocket of his suit is his wallet. On the opposite side, over his heart, is a checkbook and a pack of folded letters and notes. The outside left pocket bulges with toothpicks, breath mints, stomach-acid tablets and, you remember, the pen or pencil.

The King of Things, right?

I could tell you the history of all these things and why he carries them. But just because Charley bored me with the lecture every day for fifteen years is no reason I should bore you with it.

A few fast snatches will have to give you the picture. The pipe is because cigarettes can kill you, right? And the extra loose change is because you never just know when you have to feed a parking meter or make a phone call.

Is the picture shaping up? Do I have to give you the grooming kit lecture? Or the Don't-Lose-Your-Keys sermon?

The last thing you need is a catalog of what my father carries around with him. But no history book I know will ever give a chapter to the King of Things. And I believe somebody should sort of mention him.

If he was that much different from everybody else's old man, forget it. But Charley is Mr. Father, U.S.A.

I remember in school some movie about primitive religions. Savages and these other cats in far-off places, no civilization. They worship trees, animals, the west wind, the sun or maybe some far-out flower.

That's their bag. I don't put it down. But what Mr. Father, U.S.A., worships is Things.

The house. The mortgage he's still paying. The new car. The power mower. The color TV. The deep-freeze. The electric washer-drier. The electric can-opener. The electric garage door. The electric tooth-brush. The electric credit card in his wallet. The electric loans from the electric bank.

There's a number we do. The disk has sold over a million. We got a gold platter for it. That's right, "King of Things."

Sure you remember. We worked up a driving-type rhythm figure. Rum-a-rum, tak-tak. Rum-a-rum, tak-tak. I did it like a Dylan-type talking number, words over rhythm.

"Mister Mister running down the street;
"Mister on your stumpy little feet.
"Always braggin', dragging, grabbin' rings.
"Mister Mister, you the King of Things.

"Don't you know your heart has wings?
"You can listen when it sings.
"Feel the happiness it brings
"When you're free at last of things."

"Mister, Mister, I can tell that you can't care.
"All your running running won't get you nowhere.
"You won't listen to your heartbeat when it sings.

" 'Cause you're nothing
"When they crown you King of Things."

It's kind of funny, at that. He told me I was a bum
and I'd always be a bum. He said I'd come crawling
home for money. Only I wouldn't get any, right?

But, instead, I write this song about him. And it
sells over a million platters.

I mean, it's funny. In a gruesome way.

Let me tell you about it.

4

"You're a bum, Stanley."

His face was very pink that night. He was having
trouble with his breathing, too. This was two years
ago, dig?

He turned to my mother. All of this was in the
kitchen. We were sitting at the table and we were
supposed to be eating dinner. All the food was stuck
half-way down my throat. In a while I would have
thrown up.

"He's a bum," Charley told my mother. "What's
worse, he'll always be a bum."

My mother made a shh-ing sound. "Charley, it's bad for your digestion. You're just a little upset now. You'll feel different about it in the morning."

His blue eyes were bulging a little, he was so angry. "In the morning?" he asked her in a high voice.

"It won't look as bad in the morning."

"Yeah?" he asked. "What's going to happen between now and then? Is the four hundred bucks he blew on that crazy electric piano going to come back into his bank account?"

"It was his money, Charley. He'll put it back." My mother looked at me. "You'll turn back the piano, Stanley, won't you? You'll get the man to take it back and you'll put the money back in your account?"

"The hell I will," I said.

I know I shouldn't have said that. Even as the words came out, I knew they would blow Charley's cork higher than a kite.

Besides, it wasn't fair to my mother. I wasn't mad at her. She wasn't mad at me. So why use language on her?

But there wasn't time to think about it. The next thing I was falling backward in my chair. The back of his hand rapped me so hard across the teeth it knocked me over.

I hit the floor hard and that didn't help much, either. I jumped up and I was going to belt him one

15

in the chops. I'm taller than him and I could take him any day.

But the look on his face was so bad, I stopped dead. He looked as if he was going to have a heart attack or something. His eyes bulged and his face was the color of raspberry jello. He sounded like a locomotive trying to make it up a mountain.

I picked up the chair and put it back on all four legs. Then I sat down on it.

"Okay," I said. My lower lip had started to puff up and I knew a little blood was coming from it. But I wasn't going to let him know I cared.

"Okay, now you're going to find out what's so different about tomorrow morning."

I was a little shook up about the way my voice sounded. I mean, it was as bad as his, shaky and high and crazy. "By tomorrow morning, I'll be far away from this place and you, too," I told him. "That's what'll be different."

"Fine."

That was it. Just "fine."

I got up and started for my room. "I got packing to do," I said.

"Fine."

"Stan," my mother called.

"Let him go," Charley said. He still hadn't got his breath back. But at least his eyes had pulled in a little on their stalks.

"He's a bum," he started again, putting the needle

16

back in the groove, "and he'll never be anything but."

"You can't just let him walk out this way."

"Why not? What's the big loss?" He was losing his beet-red color now. Oh, man, he was starting to calm down real fine. "He'll be back. He'll come crawling back here some day, begging for money."

"That'll be the day," I said.

"It'll happen. And when it does, you'll get nothing from me."

I nodded. "That suits me fine," I said.

"Charley," my mother said, "he's not even nineteen yet."

"Don't worry about that," my father told her. They had begun talking about me as if I weren't there. "Wherever he goes, the draft board will track him down. And the Army will straighten him out. Or kill him in the process. So don't worry about our darling Stanley."

"Do you think they'd draft him?"

He shrugged. "Why not? College material he ain't. His grades are the worst they ever saw at Truman High."

"Except music. He always did well in music."

"I hate to see a grown woman put faith in something like that," Charley sneered. "Any idiot can carry a tune."

"But if they draft him, maybe they'll put him in the Army band."

17

"They don't have piano players in marching bands," he told her. He was right about that, of course. But it was the only thing he was right about.

"I tell you, Madge, it was a black day for us when your Aunt Tessie let us keep her piano for her. I trace the whole thing to that."

I was standing in the doorway, ready to pack my bag and leave home. I had just been rapped so hard in the teeth that my lip was bleeding. I had a lump on the back of my head where I'd hit the floor. And these two were calmly talking about me as if I'd died already.

"What was the harm?" my mother was asking. "To let a little baby play with the piano?"

"And the money we blew on piano lessons? Two bucks a week plus carfare?"

"Folks," I said.

"Tessie wanted us to enjoy the piano. She had no room for it, but as long as someone in the family could—"

"Yeah, and I blame Tessie, too."

"Folks," I said.

"You always have something nasty to blame on my side of the family," my mother started in. "As if your family didn't have plenty to answer for."

"But they didn't lend us any piano. It was like leaving a loaded gun around the house."

"Folks."

18

My mother looked up at me. "What?"

"Good-bye."

"What?"

"Good-bye."

5

☐☐☐☐☐☐☐☐☐☐☐☐☐☐☐☐

I'll level with you. I was scared green that night.

I had no idea where I was going or what I was going to live on. I had half a semester to go for graduation. I was blowing everything. In a case like that, man, you sort of run a little scared.

I threw a few things into an overnight bag, just some socks and things. The big item was the cause of my trouble, the electric piano. I could tell it was going to be a real millstone around my neck.

You have to dig the problem. I had a good enough piano at home to work out on, Aunt Tessie's. But when you gig with a group, half the time there's no piano in the hall.

Or, if there is, it's not electric. That means you wouldn't be able to make yourself heard over the guitars. Also, you can pull sounds out of an electric box that no regular piano ever made.

And, you can pack up an electric piano and travel with it. It's kind of heavy. It makes a very big suitcase. But it's portable. Which is more than you can say for the smallest regular piano.

So, naturally, as soon as I'd saved up enough, I blew it on an electric box. What else? But, like, try running away into the cold, cruel night carrying a sixty-pound suitcase. I felt like a bass-player and the piano felt like a bass fiddle loaded with lead.

But I had really had it with the home bit. The way my old man blew when I bought the box told me I had to split the scene.

I was over eighteen. Even if the draft board only gave me a few months in civvy threads, I wasn't going to blow the free time under Charley's thumb.

Anyway, out into the cold, cruel night I went, leaving the two of them arguing over their families, or something.

I got to the nearest phone booth and practically collapsed. I mean, the box was portable, all right. But it also helped if you played fullback for the Green Bay Packers.

I put in a call to Eddie Getz. He was just finishing his homework. When he heard the news he sounded scared.

"My God, Stosh," he said, "what's gonna happen?"

Eddie always talks that way. And, like most of the kids from my school, he calls me Stosh, which is Old

Country for Stanley. Or Stanley is U.S. for Stosh, which is short for Stanislas, I guess.

You don't have to know all that. Just remember your boy Stacy Nova. That's me.

On this night, I was nobody's boy. Even Eddie didn't really want any part of me. He would've asked me to stay over, but he was afraid his folks would call my folks.

"Let 'em," I said. "I'm not proud where I sleep tonight. I just don't want to sleep on any park bench, baby. Some cat will latch on to this box and I'll wake up in the morning minus four hundred bones."

"I dig, Stosh. Listen. Bring the box around. I'll keep it for you. But I can't offer to let you stay."

I thought about it for a while. It wasn't a bad offer. He'd keep the piano till I knew what I was going to do, where and how.

"Forget it, Eddie," I said. "The box and I are a team."

I didn't even know what I was talking about. Just blowing big, you know. But after I hung up I realized I had only one way to go.

I sorted out the loot in my pocket. I had three clams and change. So I walked to the nearest big intersection and waited for a cab.

I flagged him and told him to take me to one of the big Loop hotels. I rolled up to the entrance about ten minutes later and three dollars lighter.

But as I checked into the hotel, everything clicked.

I gave him the new name without a hitch. "Stacy Nova, New York City." Just like that.

I had been fooling around trying to work up a professional name for a long time. I mean, what can you do with Stosh Novotny? Anyway, it was your boy Stacy who checked in that night.

I had sixty cents left in the whole world. For a dime I bought a bag of salted peanuts at the magazine counter in the lobby.

The two quarters jingled against each other in my pants pocket. I followed the bellhop up the elevator to my room. I could see he was starting to sweat from carrying the electric piano, but I kept hands off.

Finally, he let me into the room. This was the first time in my life I'd ever done this. Are you hip to this scene, man? It's like I had been checking into expensive hotels all my life. What's more, I had thousands of bucks in my wallet to cover any emergency.

So, naturally, I gave the bellhop the two quarters. Now I was flat broke. There was nothing between me and starvation but a bag of peanuts.

6

That next week was sure a groove, baby. I nearly died.

First of all I didn't tell anybody where I was. Not even Eddie. Secondly, the hotel people were suspicious. I mean, by now they knew I didn't have anything in that big, heavy suitcase but a piano. That made me some kind of nut, right?

Worse, they hadn't seen any of my money yet, unless you count the fifty cents for the bellhop and the dime for the peanuts.

So I was kind of up-tight most of that week. I spent the time looking for work. I went to every club in town where I'd ever played or even sat and listened as a customer.

Now, Chicago has a lot of little bars and clubs and such. A lot of them have live music. It's kind of a tradition. But none of them had live groups that played my kind of bag.

Most of this live music is, like, a solo cocktail-type pianist for the tired-blood customers. You know. He sits down and rattles off a fast run on the keys. If it's autumn, he plays "September Song."

23

Like, I dig Kurt Weill. He wrote great notes. But this cocktail schmaltz is not my bag.

The other kind of live music is from Dixieland-type bands, or banjo-plunkers or soul-brother cats. Or else you get the student-type joints, coffeehouses and such, with the weirdo groups. They play this great non-music sound, wheezes and blats and moans and tinkles. Or you get folksingers. I mean, there are all kinds of bags around the Chicago scene.

But my bag in those days was straight hard rock, sort of like the Beatles started out with, or something close. And that kind of music is only for a big place with dancing.

Since then—since putting together the Flesh-Colored Bandaid and gigging around the country—my bag is a lot different. We play almost any type of joint, large or small, dancing or no dancing, older crowd, students, you name it.

But that week I was stalling the hotel for its money, man, that was something else. I mean, how does one guy get work for himself when he's really only part of a group? And the rest of the group isn't around?

So finally, it was, like Friday night. I had split from home on, maybe, a Tuesday. That's a Wednesday, Thursday and all day Friday. My stomach was so empty I could rap on it like a drum.

The only meal I was eating was breakfast because I could call down to Room Service and have it charged on my bill. But I didn't have a red cent to tip the waiter. So I figured I shouldn't stretch my luck and try for lunch or dinner.

By Friday night I was ready to take the electric box back to the man who sold it to me. I was ready to take whatever he'd shell out. Three hundred, three-fifty, anything just to have the bread to go on living.

I looked like a wild one, too. I mean, in those days I didn't have that much of a beard. I only shaved twice a week. But I was starting to come on like a junior-type hippie or something. And my one shirt didn't look too good after I'd washed it out and hung it up to dry in the hotel bathroom.

So I don't know what the manager of this one place thought when I made the scene this Friday evening.

It was a little joint on North Rush Street, a street loaded with little joints. It was about six o'clock and the place was empty. The cook was getting his dinners ready and I could smell what he was cooking.

My stomach gave a little moan and started to roll over dead. The manager of the joint gave me a funny look from behind the bar.

"If you're looking for a shot, let's see your draft card," he started out, nice, pleasant, friendly and understanding.

"I'm looking for a job, not a shot."

"Doing what?" he asked. "Haunting houses?"

He was one to talk. He was about five feet tall, give or take a half inch. And he was about five feet around. You remember that oldie, "Mr. Five by Five"? And he had so little real hair that he shaved his skull clean.

The butt of a cigar had died in one corner of his mouth. "Music," I said. My nose picked up the scent of onion soup and my stomach gave a tiny howl. "Piano."

He jerked his head at the little stand behind the bar. On it stood the smallest spinet ever made. It didn't even have a full eighty-eight-note keyboard.

"Go ahead, amaze me," he said. "Tickle the ivories a bit."

"Are you looking to hire somebody, or just putting me on?"

He shifted the cigar to the other corner of his mouth. It didn't improve his appearance at all. "Why don't you play me something and find out?"

I shrugged. My nose by now had given up on the great smells coming from the kitchen. My stomach had already died of a broken heart.

I got behind the bar, climbed up on the stand and sat down at the piano.

Now, unless you know music pretty well, you wouldn't know what a spot I was in. First, I had never played a piano like this before, a midget keyboard. Second, I was used to the electric box and the trick sounds you can get out of it. Third, I had no idea what kind of tune would please the creep with the cigar.

I settled on "Yesterday." You know, the Beatle tune. It's one of the few modern things old folks dig.

Usually I would play "Yesterday," or any other

tune, with the group. It may just have been with Eddie. Or Eddie and a drummer. The point was, I never played it as a solo except fooling around with it at home.

So I fooled around with it for him. I gave him a straight chorus. Then I gave him a big chorus with chords all over the place. Real yech. Then a small chorus, just single notes against a kind of bossa nova rhythm. Then I finished with a straight chorus again, very soft. I stopped and waited. It was very quiet in there.

"You start at nine o'clock tonight," he said.

"For how much?"

"You union?"

"No," I admitted.

"A sawbuck a night."

I frowned. Just because I wasn't a member of the musicians' union, he didn't have to pay me only ten bucks a night. When the group and I worked a dance we collected fifty dollars. That was about twelve bucks a man. Okay, but here I was carrying the whole thing as a solo. I should have gotten more than ten.

"Twenty," I rapped.

"Fifteen." He turned away from me. "That's it, buddy. Be here at nine and, for God's sake, get a clean shirt?"

"Okay."

I left the stand and came around to the front of the bar. "Uh, look," I began.

He squinted past the cigar at me. My mouth went dry and my tongue felt as if he'd tied a knot in it. He didn't say anything, either.

Then he turned and punched the "No Sale" key on the cash register. The drawer slid open and he pulled a five-buck bill out of it. He slapped it down on the bar.

"Be a big sport," he said then. "Blow yourself to a shave, too."

7

He and I never kidded each other. He knew I was only there for a while. I knew the only thing that kept me there was that he didn't have to pay me union scale.

But thanks to him, I could pay off the hotel and move to a little flea-bag furnished room near North Rush Street where I could walk to work.

I told Eddie where I was. He met me one night for dinner before I went to the club.

"I think we have to start moving, Eddie," I said to him.

I must have sounded a lot older all of a sudden. I mean, here he was, still worrying about doing his homework every night. Here I was with a new name, a job and even a room of my own.

Eddie is shorter than I am, and stubbier. He has this real kid's face. I mean even today he looks like about age twelve. He has brown eyes that get black when he's bugged.

"What do you mean, moving, Stosh?" he asked.

"Moving toward a permanent group. I think we have to find us another guitar for rhythm and a permanent drummer. And then we have to start booking real dates as a group."

Eddie's eyes were wide. "Stosh, you know I can't do that till June. My folks would murder me. I gotta graduate first."

"I'm not saying you should drop out. It's just that we have to get moving if we ever want to make it."

He gulped. "You really think we could, Stosh?"

"No question. In my spare time I'm going to start writing a few numbers. I figure by the time we whip ourselves together we ought to have at least a few songs for a demo platter."

His brown eyes got even wider. "We're going to cut a demo?"

"Sure. Why not?"

"It's expensive, Stosh. It costs hundreds of dollars."

"Leave it to me, Eddie. I'm earning pretty good now."

His face got red. "I'm paying my share," he insisted.

You have to know Eddie to understand why we've

stuck together this long. We're opposite types altogether. He's very, very square. But, man, it's refreshing.

I explained my plan. In a week or two I'd have a few numbers sketched out. We'd do a blues, very up-tempo rock-jump. And we'd do a slow number, kind of Latin and lazy.

While I was working the numbers out, I'd be earning loot for the demo. And weekends Eddie and I would pull together two other men and work on the arrangements.

Then we'd cut the demo. By that time I'd have earned enough to take off for New York and try peddling the demo to a record company. I'd also peddle the group to a booking agent.

And about graduation time, in June, when Eddie was free, we'd have enough jobs lined up to make us millionaires.

That was the plan. You have to know this business to know how insane it was. It couldn't possibly have worked. Everything was against it.

First of all, even if you have a feel for writing songs, you don't turn out two winners your first try. Second, no group that rehearses weekends with only two regulars and two fill-ins can ever be anything but lousy.

Third, New York is full of kids like me walking the streets with grubby little demo records in their grubby little hands. Fourth, I'd have enough loot to

30

last a week in New York and then I'd be stranded and broke again.

Fifth, no record company in the world will sign a group on the basis of one demo, especially when the group doesn't even exist. Sixth, no agent will book dates for a group unless he's heard their whole library, not just two numbers.

Seventh, what made me think Eddie's folks would let him leave home in June? Eighth, what gave me the idea I could eat, pay rent, buy clothes, pay for a demo, for bus fare to New York and hotel and eating money there on what I was earning?

To top off the whole crazy scheme, it was April already. We had only May and June to pull it off.

8

I won't make any mystery about it. By June I was up to my eyeballs in debt. There was no group. There were no numbers. There was no demo.

All I had to show for my trouble was three things. I'd joined the union. I'd moved on to another joint where I got paid better. And I'd met a whole bunch of new friends who turned me on to pot.

If you don't dig the whole pot scene, what happened won't make too much sense to you.

First of all, you read a lot about high school kids smoking pot. I mean, like, the papers and magazines are full of scare stories. Judges are always lecturing kids. You know.

But the funny thing was, most of the kids at my school were clean. I don't know why that was. I mean, either the stories in the papers were wrong, or the kids at my school were very backward.

Anyway, we knew a few kids who turned on with pot. But it wasn't anything to get revved up about. I remember I smoked a joint one night at a dance we were playing. Some girl came backstage at intermission and she was holding grass.

So Eddie and I shared a joint she gave us and, like, nothing. I mean nothing. But that was when we were sophomores.

When I joined the union, I got too expensive for the place I was working. But, by then, Stacy Nova was a name along North Rush Street. So I moved two blocks north to another place.

These three people used to fall by almost every night. I wasn't sure who was what. There were two guys and a girl, all a little older than I was. They worked in the same ad agency on the Near North Side. They all lived in the neighborhood and they were real tight buddies.

Pretty soon I was one of them. They would call out numbers for me to play and by now I could cocktail-piano with the best of them. I didn't know half the tunes they liked, oldies by Gershwin and Cole Porter and Irving Berlin. So I laid hands on a fake book.

This is strictly illegal, of course. It's a book crammed with the melodies of songs and the chords that go with them.

You're supposed to buy each song from the publisher, so the writers get paid, too. But these illegal fake books give you what you need. You save all the money you might have spent on regular sheet music.

With the fake book, there was no stopping Stacy-baby. I mean, these new friendly cats would call out "I Concentrate on You" or "Miss Otis Regrets" or "How Long Has This Been Going On?" or some other real oldie. And there I would be with my little fake book, knocking out the tune and keeping the people happy.

That was another thing I was learning. I could fake tunes now. Faking is what musicians call it when you don't really know a tune, but you sort of play it by ear and fill in chords as you go along. I never used to be able to do that.

Now, man, I could fake with the best. This new place I was working at stayed open a little later than the other one. I was starting at nine, but I was playing till after one in the morning on week nights and a lot later on Fridays and Saturdays. I slept late during the day.

This is not the best way to try to write new songs or rehearse them. As a matter of fact, the only way you can do that is if you use real will power. And, by then, I had other things to do with what spare time I had.

The girl's name was Frankie. I guess she started off in life as Frances but she wanted everyone to call her Frankie.

She lived about five blocks from the club in a pad that looked like the year 2001, all see-through plastic and chrome. And as far as grass was concerned, this chick was holding a pound and then some.

She used to take her vacation in two blasts, two weeks in Europe during the summer and a week in Acapulco at Christmas.

I think she had her connection down south of the border. Anyway, she had muggles coming out of her ears, Acapulco Brown and Guadalajara Green. The air in that pad was always blue.

She called it by its Spanish-Indian name, which is "moteh," and she seemed to have cornered the Midwest market. I mean, like everybody and his dog took from Frankie.

"You a pusher, baby?" I asked her once.

She looked hurt. "Man, I just wanna turn the whole world on," she said. "If you ain't got no bread, man, you take free from little Frankie."

This is a chick that graduated some girls' college you all heard of in the East.

But talked real funky, you know, all kinds of wanna and ain't and gotta and like that. Exactly the way Stacy Nova was trying not to talk. Dig?

I'll say this for Frankie. She was always good for a touch. If you needed ten or even a hundred, Frankie would get it up for you.

And pretty. I shouldn't forget pretty. I'm kind of tall, maybe six feet. But in her heels, Frankie was just as tall.

She told me once, when she was high, that it was a bad scene being tall if you were a chick. I didn't see it. I mean, she had a lot of guys around her. Not just juvenile delinquent piano players like me. Real heavy-holding cats, copywriters in ad agencies and art directors with big mustaches and like that. You know: they all drove sports cars.

Well, being tall didn't seem to cool any of these cats. They kept Frankie swinging every night, seven nights straight. I know. She used to fall by the club where I was playing. No matter who she was out with, she'd bring them by the club to dig me.

At first I thought she did it to make me jealous. I mean, I admit it. I had a thing for Frankie. She turned me on, not only to pot, but to life, sort of.

So when she'd bring these studs around just about closing time every night, I would get real jealous and try to cool her and them.

But with a chick like Frankie, you had to be out of your skull to think any one guy had the inside track. She was a new-type chick. She had no idea of getting married and settling down. Yet.

After I dug what she was, I stopped being jealous. But I still liked her.

And I liked her grass.

I suppose that was the whole problem that summer.

9

You have to know pot to know what happened that spring and summer. To know why I never did make it to New York with the big demo platter that would mean success for Eddie Getz and me.

Now, you have heard all kinds of things about pot.

It depends who's talking. Some put pot down real hard. I mean, like, man, they slam it bad. Some think it's the greatest. They are as hard to believe as the mammas who put it down.

The ones who bad-name grass are two kinds. One kind knows what they're talking about but tells you lies "for your own good." The other people don't know what they're talking about at all. Nohow.

They tell you it's habit-forming and you know it isn't. They tell you it makes you do things that hurt yourself and other people. Booze does the same thing —maybe worse—but you don't see anybody closing up the juice shops.

They tell you pot leads to drugs, and then on to speed and yellowjackets and acid and even hard junk like H and M.

Well, you know it doesn't do that any more than water leads to drowning. What I mean is, a cat who wants to fight off the world with pot is going to find it isn't up to that kind of work.

So he has to move on to strong stuff. It's H and meth and acid that let you fold up the world and tuck it away in a drawer somewhere and forget it. Grass won't do that.

Like water: if you want to drink it, fine. If you want to swim in it, fine. But if you want to kill yourself in it, it'll drown you real good.

If you know that much about pot, you know that the johns who put it down are telling you lies. But if you really know pot, you know the grassheads are freaked-out, too.

I mean, you talk to real diehard grassheads. To them the world begins and ends with pot. It cures everything. A pot high is the greatest thing in life. So they have to share. And all that.

That's how Frankie came on with me. I mean, when she first dug me, she figured, well, here's a real swinger, jazz musician-type. He must be holding grass like the U.S. Mint holds nickels.

But, as I told you, nobody in my school made that scene too much. So the first time I really settled down to smoke a few joints in peace and quiet was at Frankie's pad on the Near North Side.

A devout grasshead will tell you it's hard to describe a pot high. Wrong. Anybody can describe a pot high, his own high. But it won't be the same as somebody else's.

It's a lot like a whiskey high, only freakier. With the sauce, you usually go the same route: numb gums, thick tongue, then dizzy and sick, then out. Pow. Sleepsville.

Grass isn't always the same. First you get a little high, a little excited. Things look brighter and sound quicker. Jokes are funnier. People are nicer. So far, it's like booze.

Then you start to float. You know you're high, but you also know you're floating. It's still like a good whiskey high.

About your third or fourth stick of boo, you start spinning. You can feel your own skin. It's weird. I mean, normally, you never get a real feeling from your skin unless somebody pinches it or something.

But now you feel your skin kind of creep or tingle or something. And whatever you do now seems as if it's the smartest, smoothest, neatest, quickest, happiest thing you ever did. Then, out. Pow. Sleepsville.

Sounds like a booze high, right? But next morning it's different. No hangover.

Now, what I described is just a high, right? It's not the end of the world. It's not some new religion. It's not a crusade or a new way of life or any other wild thing grassheads claim for it.

It's just a way of getting high, if that's your scene.

But, with my luck, it took me most of that summer to find out what I know now. It took me all summer to find out that pot is just something people use to kill time.

It took me all summer—when I should have been getting on with my music—to learn that you float, all right. And while you float and lose track of time, the world is moving right along without you.

By September, Eddie Getz was so mad he could hardly say one decent word to me. Which was nothing to how I felt about myself.

I looked back on that summer, smoking up a storm in Frankie's pad, as one long nothing, which it was. One nice long nothing.

"I got to cut out, baby," I told Frankie one morning.

I usually slept till after lunch, because of my late working hours. But she had to be at her office no later than ten. So our morning talks were never anything great on sweetness and light.

"I got to get away from you and grass and the whole scene," I told her.

She had bought this wild new hat. It was the color

of strawberry ice cream. It was shaped like one of these Australian bush hats, the brim up on one side.

She was standing in front of the mirror, adjusting the hat. I was sitting there staring at her. Or trying to. My eyes didn't focus too well on so little sleep.

"So go," she said.

I mean, like this chick was Cool City, U.S.A., right? "I will," I said. "As of now, today. We split, dig?"

"Dig."

She gave the brim of her hat a little extra tug and walked right out of my life. Like that.

Three months up in smoke. Grass smoke.

10

It was that blown summer, with nothing to show for it, that almost busted me up with Eddie Getz.

"You let that Frankie chick make a fool out of you," he told me one day.

This was late in August some time. The hot summer air baked slowly over Chicago. Whenever some of it drifted out over Lake Michigan, it picked up a little extra humidity. Then it drifted back again to keep us unhappy. I was lying on the bed, gasping.

"How did she do that?" I asked Eddie.

We were sitting around my pad late in the afternoon. I had a few hours yet before I started working.
Eddie was out of work completely. I think that was
what was making him jump so salty.

"How?" he asked. "You blew the whole summer on
that chick and you don't even know how she made a
fool of you?"

"I got a few jollies out of it."

"You got nothing to show but a bunch of dead sticks
of grass."

"Man, you square," I put him on. "A butt of pot is
called a roach, baby. Don't you know anything?"

"That's what I mean," Eddie snapped. "All you
learned all summer is what to call a smoked-out butt.
Instead of getting to New York and stirring up
a storm."

"But I've got my memories," I said, giving him a
big, fake wink.

He made a face. "She didn't look that great to me,"
he muttered. "Anyway," he went on suddenly, "what
really bugs me is that you're getting ready to blow the
fall, too."

He was beginning to get under my skin a little and
I guess I started to show it. I mean, after all, whose
idea was it to make a demo and take it to New York?

"If I want to delay my own plans, baby," I told him,
"whose business is it besides mine?"

"Okay." He stood up. His eyes looked very black.
"I dig. So long." He started for the door.

I closed my eyes. He could be annoying some time. "Eddie, will you stop it?"

"What do you want me to do? Sit around here listening to you make excuses?" I opened my eyes to find that he had the door open. He was starting out into the hall.

"Or maybe," he was saying, "I should sit around listening to how you were going to make the demo all by yourself." He gave me a disgusted look. "You been playing solo piano too long. Solo piano and pot duet. Your brains have drained."

I waved a hand at him. "You're jealous."

I figured that was the only way to keep him from lamming out on me. Eddie gets stubborn streaks some times. If he says good-bye he means it. But one thing he can't stand is being accused of something that isn't so.

"Jealous of what? Your big job? Okay," he admitted, "I wish I was working, too. But what else should I be jealous of? At least I have my diploma. And I'm not living in some roach-hole off canned chili."

He jerked his thumb at the top of my dresser. Well, you know, the way I had been spending my summer, I was kind of eating on the run. I mean, the club where I worked was always good for a few sandwiches during the evening. But for other meals, I faked it.

I mean, I was still hooked on salted peanuts. I always had a few stashed away in the pad. And once in a while I would buy a can of something at the local deli and heat it up.

That's what bugged Eddie. I had this little electric iron upside-down on the dresser, propped on a telephone book. And there was an empty can of chili con carne on the iron.

You can heat up a can of chili that way in just under ten minutes. But always remember to open it before you heat it. First time I forgot. When I did, it shot these big jets of red-hot chili all over the walls.

"It isn't as if you couldn't afford to eat in a decent place," Eddie said.

He was still posing in the doorway, giving the rest of the tenants down the hall a playback of my life, free of charge.

"What have you been doing with your loot anyway?" he asked. He had finally hooked himself on his own question. "What do you spend it on?"

"Well," I said, waving a hand at the chili-spattered walls. "There's the rent for this place."

"Whatever they charge you, it's a felony."

"And clothes."

"Clothes?" he stepped over to the one and only closet in the place. Instead of a door, it had a curtain on a string. He swept open the curtain.

If I do say so myself, it had a few good sets of threads hanging there. And no El Cheapo's, either.

"The cleaning bills alone would flatten any normal person," I put in.

"I dig." Eddie went back to the doorway position again. "Rent, clothes, and pot. Beautiful. Okay. Over and out."

He started to close the door behind him. In another second he would have gone for good. I hopped up off the bed and grabbed his arm.

"Okay. Cool it, baby. You win."

He turned back and gave me one of those are-you-for-real looks. "Meaning what?"

I shrugged. "Meaning whatever I said at first. We cut the demo and I take it to New York. Can you find us another guitar man and a drummer?"

He came back in the room and sat down on the edge of the bed. "I got a few in mind. But you have to hear them before we choose one." He thought for a minute. "You got any numbers for the demo."

"Don't worry," I told Eddie. "By the time we put a combo together, I'll have the numbers."

11

The end of August was a bad time for me. The weather was muggy and hot all the time. I was feeling depressed a lot. I tried to figure out why I was so bugged.

I mean, things weren't that bad. I had a steady job. Eddie and I had picked up two good men. We were rehearsing three afternoons a week. I was saving money for the New York trip. I should have been happy.

I ran into Frankie only once. It was around Labor Day, the early part of September. She dropped by the club with not one but two new guys. She stiffed me solid.

So, when I finished a set, instead of going back to the dressing room, I passed by her table on my way to the bar. I nodded politely to her.

"Hey, man," one of the cats with her said. "You play great notes."

He turned to Frankie. "You didn't tell me you knew him."

"Do I?" she asked.

It had all the signs of the start of something bad. So I cut out to the dressing room. When I started the next set, she and the two cats were gone. I really felt lousy.

Maybe I missed her. Maybe I missed the pot.

Grassheads swear pot won't let you down. I think maybe it does. I think if you go off it, you start to get the grims.

It's nothing serious, like kicking H cold turkey. Anybody can go off pot. But I think you have to be ready to feel lousy about life for a while.

If you can get through that without lighting up a

joint or two, then you know you're one of the lucky ones who can take it or leave it.

Anyway, I was a working fool. I knocked off not two but four sides. And Eddie and I cooked up the kind of sound that we wanted for a trademark.

I suppose you know what a trademark is. I mean, everything has one, from a bottle of beer to a truck. Combos have trademarks, too. They call it a new sound.

It's a matter of playing around with what you have to work with. You make it sound enough different so people will recognize it next time they hear it.

It's no secret that most pop music is written for a real tin-ear audience. I mean, that's why so many of the numbers sound alike. They are alike. They have the same three or four chords. Your little baby brother could learn to play them in half a day.

It was the Beatles that started mixing up wild new chords and blowing everybody's mind. After them, every new group had to make it with a new sound, a new trademark.

Ours was kind of nice. You have to remember this was over a year ago. By now, our thing has been copied so many ways you probably don't even remember it was ours first.

The best way to describe it is to call it a samba-rock. Does that give it to you? It's like the bossa nova tempo with a strong rock beat.

Also the voicing of the instruments is different. The

bass guitar hits his notes so low you hardly hear what the note is, you feel it. The drum keeps off his bass as much as possible. He makes it with the hi-sock cymbal and the temple blocks and rim-shots and like that.

But the biggest thing about our style was something nobody could copy for a long time. You had to play together as long as Eddie and I had to pull it off.

In the music books it's called counterpoint. Sometimes Eddie would carry the melody. I would weave around it with another tune, just a little different.

Sometimes I would carry the melody and Eddie would supply the other part. Sometimes we'd trade back and forth inside of one number. You weren't sure where the melody was or even what it was.

And I would rap out those sharp little staccato chords that give you the extra Brazilian flavor.

It was a gas and a half. For nearly a year it was all ours, our thing, our trademark.

But I'm getting ahead of myself.

12

About the middle of September, I had saved enough money for the demo session. Eddie had picked up a few jobs with groups around town, strictly Saturday night gigs, and he coughed up a few sawbucks, too.

We wanted to tape the four numbers we'd rehearsed. But we knew we could only afford to have two of them pressed as a demo record.

One was a real head-on treatment of our new style, working over the old Stones' number, "Satisfaction." No vocal. Another was a new thing I wrote called "Dead Abe." It was then and it still is my all-time best.

You know how the notes on a piano go? Well, if you play D,E,A,D,A,B,E, you get the melody of the song.

If that isn't sick enough for you, dig this: I took the melody on the piano in C, but Eddie was in E, a third above me, and the bass guitar was making the scene in A, a third below me.

Man, it was Wild City. Everybody hated it, including Eddie.

The third number was another original, a little love-type thing I called "Grassy Day." It was all about this cat remembering this chick and all the grassy days they had together.

It gave Eddie the fits. "You still haven't got that Frankie chick out of your skull, man," he said.

The fourth side was "King of Things." I didn't want to cut it at all. I hated it once I heard how it came out. But Eddie and the other boys liked it.

Well, all right. Now for a little lesson in the music business.

We had these four numbers on tape. At the prices

we were paying, they had to be good. Any halfway decent recording studio with good equipment and engineers who know what they're doing is going to run you at least a C-note an hour.

That's a hundred clams, baby, and it takes at least four hours to tape four sides the way you want them.

The good studios want a big fat cash deposit before they even let you set foot near their mikes. I guess in the early days of rock they had had a few groups who cut sides and stiffed them for the rent.

So, right off the bat, Eddie and I had shelled out close to four hundred bucks. And all we had to show was a tape of two songs everybody liked, one everybody but me hated, and one everybody liked but me.

Now, when it comes to making a demo, the next thing that rears up and bites you in the pocket is the need for a lot more cash.

See, you have this tape. Fine. But now they have to make 45 rpm. records from it, the little ones with the big holes in the middle. And that is going to cost you.

So you can see that with all that loot riding on it, Eddie and I had to be pretty careful which two we'd press on the demo disk.

I wanted "Dead Abe" and "Grassy Days." Clean-cut decision, right? And Eddie was just as good at making up his mind. He wanted "Satisfaction" and "King of Things."

That was only the latest of the five million arguments he and I have had. We never see eye to eye and

49

we never will. But it doesn't shake us up a whole lot.

So we split the difference. I got the one I loved and everybody hated. He got the one I hated and everybody loved, "Dead Abe" for me, "King of Things" for Eddie.

That brought us directly to the bottom of our pockets. There wasn't a dime left for anything else, including food.

It was almost October and the weather had cooled off nicely. I was getting dressed to go to the club and I tightened my belt and found I could pull it in a notch to a whole new hole.

"I'm starving to death," I reported to Eddie.

"I'll bring you some food from home," he promised. "Uh, by the way. . . ."

His voice died away. It usually does when he has something to say that he doesn't want to say. "By the way," he repeated, "I ran into your folks last night."

"No kidding." I tied my tie and started to swab a rag over my shoetops.

"They wanted to know how you were and where you were."

"But you didn't tell them."

"Uh, no."

Now Eddie cannot lie. I mean, he can try, but it never works. "You mean you really didn't tell them? Because the last thing I need is one of them busting in here. I'm still a minor, legally. They can cross me up good if they feel like it."

"Uh, well." He stopped and thought about everything. "I said I hadn't seen you around lately. That wasn't much of a lie because I hadn't seen you all yesterday, right?"

"Go ahead, spill it."

"So your mother said 'How's his health?' And I said 'Not bad.' And she said—"

"She said, 'If you haven't seen him around lately how do you know how his health is?' " I finished for him. "Boy, are you slow."

"I didn't tell them, Stosh, honest I didn't."

"So what did the old man say?"

"Nothing. He gave me a look and pulled your mother away."

"Sounds like him." I threw down the shoe rag. I wasn't angry or anything, not even faintly disturbed. But I threw it down so hard it hit an empty glass and knocked it off the chair. It smashed on the floor.

"Now look," Eddie said. He started to pick up the sharp splinters.

"Leave them."

"They'll cut you."

"So I'll bleed," I said.

I left him on his knees picking up the silly splinters. I wasn't really angry. I slammed the door when I left.

13

You'll wonder why all of this took so long. I mean, when you read about it in fan books, it seems to take overnight, bums to heros in the snap of a finger.

But the plain fact was I'd left home in June. Here it was October and all I had to show for my big move was a few hundred feet of brown magnetic tape.

I decided I had to make money faster. Eddie had to make more, too. So we sold ourselves as a duo to a new club on the Near North Side. This was in an area called Old Town.

In Chicago, like most anywhere else, all the old nice-looking buildings have been torn down. In their place are all these glass things that look like matchboxes on end. It's the same everywhere.

So in this part of town they decided to make it look like the good old days again. Maybe people who were sick and tired of looking at glass matchboxes would flock around.

They did. We auditioned for this place in Old Town that was down an alley. So, of course, it was called Alky Lane, as if this were the 1920's and the joint a prohibition speakeasy.

They had to explain it to me, too. There was a time in this country when it was against the law to make or sell booze. So the gangsters took over the booze business and people kept right on drinking. Usually they went to these illegal places called speakeasies.

This hefty guy who ran Alky Lane liked our sound. We were doing with guitar and piano some of the stuff we had first worked out for a four-piece combo. I used the regular piano in the joint, not my electric one. The numbers were quiet. They sounded groovy to us. The big guy dug them, too.

"You boys are great," he said. "A hundred and fifty a week."

I gave him a pained look. "What?"

"Apiece," he added.

So we reported for work two nights later. We had a beautiful crowd. They were in their twenties and thirties and they were with us solid. But some time after midnight the audience would always start to change.

We'd start getting these older guys showing up in fives and tens, whole bunches of them with badges on their lapels. They were from out of town, usually, and they were in Chicago for a convention. And somebody had told them Alky Lane was a real hot spot.

So they showed up looking for chicks and wanting to sing the old-time songs like "Heart of My Heart" and "I'll Tell You My Dream" and "Carolina Moon" and "Down by the Old Mill Stream" and all the rest.

Eddie and I couldn't even stand to listen to it, much less play it.

Well, the first week, the owner stayed straight. I mean, he stuck by us and by the crowd that showed up early and dug our sound.

But it was easy to see that the early birds didn't have the loot. I mean, they would stretch a beer for an hour. By midnight, these middle-aged tigers started padding in looking for blood. They were ready to spend cash like it was going out of style.

So, guess what?

By the third week the hefty owner had imported chicks. Right. Four chicks were hustling drinks at the bar and rumpling the tigers' bald heads. They were up on the bandstand in their little tiny bikini-shorts and long lace stockings go-go dancing.

Now, I have nothing against girls in bikinis go-go dancing. It's just that when they dance, I don't like to play. I like to watch, right? And I don't like to spend the time in between playing "Sweet Adeline" and "Peg O My Heart" and "By the Light of the Silvery Moon."

So, it wasn't more than a month before this very nice place, where we could do our thing and have people like it, was just another grind joint for toothless tigers with money. Let me tell you about it.

We'd been at Alky Lane six weeks. I had met a new girl who seemed a little different from the others. It was her first week. Her name was Carol and she came from Ottumwa, Iowa.

I mean Ottumwa, Iowa. Dig?

She was a gorgeous girl, but you couldn't tell at first. She had this dead white hair hanging down in sick Shirley Temple curls. She had double false eyelashes on her upper lids and single ones on the bottom.

She came to work the sixth week and I latched onto her the night she showed up. I barged in the girls' dressing room right after the first set.

I don't mean it was really a dressing room. Not in a box like Alky Lane. It was the manager's office where he kept a safe and spare menus and light bulbs and packages of paper towels and great scenic stuff like that.

In this room, which was about six feet square, four girls had to change, make up, rest and whatever else go-go girls who hustle drinks do.

But we had to earn loot. As soon as we'd collected enough to buy a dozen demo disks and leave me expense money, we would quit.

In Chicago there is a type of girl called a B-Girl. She gets out with the customers and blinks her eyes. They say, "What'll you have, cutie?" She tells them champagne or scotch or whatever the most expensive drink is.

The bartender gives her a glass with a little water

in it. The water is slightly brown. The bartender has put a little tea or coke in it. And he charges the sucker a few bucks for the girl's champagne or whatever she asked for.

These girls who hustle drinks sometimes end up going home with one of the suckers. In the end, after they lose their looks, that's about the only way they can earn a living.

But this Carol was brand new. She didn't even know how to hustle Drink One. That was what attracted me to her at first.

I saw her out there struggling with a handy John who wanted to buy her champagne. "I don't like it," she said.

"Whatever you want, baby. Name your poison."

"Ginger ale," Carol said.

Several customers nearby fainted, or something. But what can you expect from a girl from Ottumwa, Iowa, who'd been in Chicago all of one week.

I barged into her dressing room right after the first set. I looked around for her but she was gone.

There was a new chick that looked a little like her, though. She had the same goofy eye makeup. But she had short black hair. Then I saw this Shirley Temple wig hanging on the chair.

"Stand back and let me kill it," I said, menacing the wig.

It looked like a very sick animal of some rare kind that would never get well. Carol laughed, I told her who I was and then invited her out back for a smoke.

There was a little sort of fire-escape balcony behind Alky Lane. It looked out over a part of the Chicago River that ran past. Overhead we could hear the sound of auto horns and traffic noise from Michigan Avenue. I guess we were actually down under the avenue in some little pocket.

A barge was moving slowly on the river, little red lights on all four corners. "Welcome to Chicago," I told the barge.

"How did you know I was new in town?" Carol asked.

I figured out her confusion and decided to let it stand. "Anybody who's hired to hustle drinks and orders ginger ale has got to be from the sticks."

She blinked a few times, fast. "It's Ottumwa, Iowa. And I wasn't hired to hustle drinks. I was hired as a dancer. That's what the ad said."

She had a very nice face. It was a little round, not like Frankie's at all. Frankie's had been long and lean. Carol's was—not fat or even plump—just rounder and friendlier. She had eyes the size of baseballs, even without her makeup.

I reached over and pulled off one of her lower fake eyelashes. "You look foolish," I said. "Who does your makeup?"

She snatched back the eyelash. "Me. Did I criticize your playing?"

"No."

"Well, it's cornball."

I nodded. "You're so right, baby."

So we talked about our troubles. We'd both been hired under false pretenses. Then it was time for another set and we went back to work.

Anyway, I was going to tell you about the night Eddie and I quit.

It was the end of that sixth week, Carol's first week in town. We had collected barely enough for the demos and my New York expenses. We figured we had to stick it out a few more weeks to be absolutely safe.

It was Saturday night, our busy time. It was well after one A.M. The joint, as the old song says, was jumping. All the tigers were growling. The colored water was flowing freely. Carol was up there with the other girls shaking away to this idiot go-go stuff Eddie and I were playing.

After the set, Carol started to cut out for the rear balcony. We met there as often as we could. The big owner clamped his heavy hand on her arm.

"Get out there and drink, baby," he told her. "And none of that ginger ale jazz, okay?"

"Maybe she doesn't feel like it," I suggested politely.

He turned to look at me. This was not the usual run-of-the-mill-type owner. He was younger than average and bigger than most. I figured him to be about thirty-five.

You hear rumors anywhere you work. The rumor about Mr. Muscles was he wasn't the real owner of Alky Lane. He was fronting for owners who didn't like to show their faces in public too much if they could help it.

You get a lot of joints like that in Chicago. Elsewhere, too.

"Maybe she doesn't feel like working here any more," Muscles told me. "And maybe you don't either."

I shrugged. It might have been all right to blow my own job, but not to blow Carol's for her. So all I did was shrug.

"Get out there and mix and mingle, baby. And drink up a storm," he told her.

Carol gave me a look. "I wasn't hired for that," she told him.

"Okay," the owner-front-man said. "But that's what I'm paying you for."

"I don't get it," Carol said.

"Come payday you won't either," he said.

She turned to me. "Will you explain this, Stacy?"

I shrugged again. "Most of the girls get paid by the drink. Like, if you hustle a dozen drinks a night, you collect twelve bucks."

"But what about what I get for dancing?"

I looked at Muscles. "What'll she get paid for the week?"

It was his turn to shrug. "At this point I figure she's

59

hustled enough booze to earn herself a whole dollar."

"That isn't fair," Carol burst out. "There's a law against you doing that to me."

"A law?" Muscles laughed. "A law for B-broads like you? Did you ever hear anything like it?" he asked me. "This tramp thinks there's a law to protect hookers like her."

I had just about stopped growing that year. I was a little under six feet tall and thanks to not squandering my money on food I weighed about 150. I was skinny. Muscles stood about six-three and I figure he weighed in at about 210, no flab.

So I shrugged again.

Carol started to cry. "What kind of names are those to call me?" she sobbed.

I could feel my throat tighten, as if I were sobbing, too. I looked at her and then I looked at Muscles. I was nineteen and he was 35. I figured he knew every dirty trick there was.

Carol's mascara was streaking down her face. "You can't call me that," she was crying. A crowd had gathered around us.

"Be happy I didn't call you what you really are," Muscles glared at her.

So I hit him over the head with a barstool.

What happened after that was gorgeous.

First off, let me say that I put everything I had into that barstool. It weighed a good ten pounds on its own and I lifted it about as high over my head as I could. And I really leaned into it, too.

Oh, man, sheer beauty. He let out a yelp and fell in a little heap on the floor, trying to grab at my legs and spill me over.

All of a sudden a man wearing a badge that read "Hi, there, I'm Ed Czermat from Amalgamated Fudge, Ltd." grabbed my arm.

"You young hooligan!" he screamed. "Juvenile delinquent!"

"Hippie!" somebody else yelled.

Then a young guy in back, wearing a badge that said "Hello, my name is Matt Prohaska of Chillicothe Tool. What's Yours?" hauled off and socked Ed Czermat in the stomach.

A bald man with metal-rimmed glasses gave a squeak like a scared mouse and fell off his barstool on top of Muscles, who was trying to get up off the floor. Down went Muscles again.

Two elderly women came to Ed Czermat's rescue and began hitting Matt Prohaska on the head with their handbags. This got one of the go-go girls mad. She emptied a pitcher of water on their permanents.

Then it really started.

I didn't wait. I grabbed Eddie with one hand and Carol with the other and we busted out the back way, onto the little balcony and down the fire escape stairs to the lower level of Michigan Avenue.

"My guitar!" Eddie yelped.

"My clothes!" Carol howled.

We figured the only one of us who could risk going back was Eddie. He returned fifteen minutes later with his guitar, Carol's coat and the start of a black eye.

Which was how we quit and I started on the high road to fame, fortune and starvation in New York City.

14

I don't know how well you dig the Chicago scene. Back in the 1920's it was Gang City. But that all died out with Al Capone.

So they say. All Eddie and I knew was what anybody who grew up in Chicago knows. If you tangle with a guy you suspect is hooked up with the mob, you have only two choices. Settle up or blow town.

I had no idea if Mr. Muscles was really a front man for the mob. You never know a thing like that, ever.

On the other hand, it's kind of stupid to stand around waiting to find out. The newspapers are full of guys who waited around to see if they were right.

What's one more news story about a hit-and-run

killing? Or about somebody jumping out of a window?

And then, too, what could you do to settle up with the mob for clobbering one of their boys with a bar stool?

I mean, besides tell them you're very sorry.

So we packed fast. We dropped Carol at her pad and came back for her in forty minutes flat. Somehow Eddie had conned his father into letting him use the family heap. All three of us piled into it and hit the expressway for O'Hare Airport.

Eddie's idea was to leave the car in a parking lot and mail the ticket to his folks—from New York.

We figured, what the heck, O'Hare is one of the busiest airports in the world. There has to be a bunch of planes going in and out all the time.

But not at three A.M.

We had our choice. We could wait around till about eight A.M. for a flight to New York. This more or less guaranteed that if anybody was looking for the three of us, they had five whole hours to score.

Besides, even if we made the eight A.M. flight, it wasn't any protection against being nabbed. Eddie and I had done a lot of talking around the joint. Muscles knew we planned to head for New York some day soon.

So we did the only smart thing we could. I bought Carol a one-way ticket to Ottumwa, Iowa, on an airline I never heard of. She went in the ladies room to wait the hour or so before her flight left.

63

Meanwhile, Eddie and I looked over the possibilities. A flight from Washington, D.C., was due in about the time Carol flew out. This D.C. flight had already stopped at Pittsburgh and Cleveland. It was due to turn south and stop at Nashville, Memphis, Dallas and Phoenix before it limped into Los Angeles.

I don't know if you've ever been on the lam.

It looks very exciting and glamorous when you see it on TV. I mean, this guy is being hunted and he has all these great adventures. But they never catch him. He lives to star in next week's show all over again.

Sorry to disappoint. It isn't like that at all. What it's like is horrible. I mean, you jump every time there's any loud noise. You think everybody's watching you. You sit there and look innocent. But all you look like is a bank robber.

Every time somebody said something over the loudspeaker, I expected them to call our names. Every time anybody walked by our bench, I expected them to pull a gun on us.

We may have waited a regular sixty-minute hour. But it lasted sixty years.

Two things made it worse. One was that we weren't at all sure that we were wanted by anybody. It made me feel a little foolish, sitting there like a scared rabbit, if the mob wasn't really after us. But we couldn't take the chance.

64

The second was that I couldn't talk to Carol. I mean, if the boys were looking for us, they would expect her to be with us. So it made sense to keep her out of sight.

But it would have helped a lot if I could have talked to her. There were a lot of things I could have worked out. The first one would have been why I went so overboard on her that I belted Muscles with a stool.

The flight to Ottumwa came in and I guess Carol could hear them announce it in the ladies room. She came out, carrying a zipper case. It held all she had in the world, I guess. Her one-week adventure in the big city was over.

I left Eddie on the bench and went to the departure lounge where Carol was heading. There were two people waiting for the flight. They looked like ordinary people. So I sat down as if I were taking the flight, too. Carol showed up a second later and sat down next to me.

"When will I see you again?" she asked. "Or will I?"

She was looking straight ahead. If somebody was watching us with binoculars she didn't want them to know she knew me.

"I'll write you when I get set."

"Please?"

"You know I will, baby."

She shook her head. "No, I don't. Why should you want to see me again? After all the trouble I caused you?"

I shrugged and took her hand. If anybody was watching us with binoculars, they sure would have been fooled. How could they ever tell we knew each other?

"I'm telling you," I said. "I'll write you from New York first thing."

What I wasn't telling her was that our plane wasn't going to New York.

15

I suppose everybody knows about Nashville.

Or thinks they do. You ask the average with-it teen-ager and he may remember John Sebastian's "Nashville Cats," a groovy side. Or he gives you a funny look:

"Nashville? Squaresville? Corn City?"

Nashville is where country music's at. I mean, when the record says the town is full of guitar pickers, each one better than the next, that's sure enough what they mean.

We had left O'Hare Airport after four-thirty in

the morning. An hour later the sun was just touching the tops of these rolling hills down below.

In those days I didn't know from plane trips. I think I'd taken one or two in my whole life. So the sight of these terrific hills down below was something else, man.

I mean, this was it. There was some kind of river looping around between the hills. And in the distance I could see this city built right on the hills.

A few minutes later Eddie and I were walking through the airport terminal. We had a lot on our minds. But the first thing we had to figure out was simple: what did we do now?

You see, the main thing was to blow Chicago. Okay, we did that. And the second thing was not to go so far it used up a lot of money. Okay, Nashville filled the bill.

But what then?

Now, I used to read the fan magazines as much as you. I mean, I read all those groovy, swinging interviews with groovy, swinging people.

I know how the magazines make it look. To them all these cats have top talent. And it's talent that gets these cats to the top. True?

Well, maybe.

But I'm here to say that if you don't have luck, you can have all the talent in the world and not make it. Look what happened to us in Nashville.

Up till now, I wouldn't say Stacy Nova had made

much of a splash. I had been working pretty steady. Eddie and I had a handful of good numbers. And we had a demo tape.

But we hadn't set anybody's world on fire. Aside from a few barflies and such on Chicago's Near North Side who'd ever heard of us?

We were two underage musicians with about five hundred bucks between us, alone in a city where we knew nobody. And the mob was looking for us.

How's that for openers?

So we waited around for some kind of airport bus and there wasn't any at that hour. Eddie mailed the O'Hare parking ticket to his folks in Chicago. We had a cup of coffee. We were low.

"You boys waiten faw a plane?" the waitress asked.

She was about a year older than us, maybe nineteen or twenty. She had just about the perkiest voice we'd heard all night.

I shook my head. "We're not sure yet."

She eyed Eddie's guitar case. "I can tell you're not from around heah," the waitress said. "You looken faw work?"

I started to shake my head again. After all, it wasn't work we wanted. It was New York.

But Eddie had other ideas. I asked him later why he said what he said. He told me he figured we were better off not getting to New York so fast. He figured the mob might forget about us if we dropped out of sight for a while.

68

"That's right," he piped up. "You know of any work?"

The waitress smiled. "Faw a guitah pickah in Nashville?"

All three of us laughed. I suppose if there was one thing Nashville didn't need it was one more guitah pickah.

Now, get the picture. It's six in the morning. This girl had never laid eyes on us before in her entire young life. We are two seedy strangers from Strangersville, U.S.A.

So she ripped off a blank ticket from her ticket-pad and scribbled a name and address on it.

"Heah," she said, handing it to me. "You go see this man first thang today."

See what I mean about luck?

16

Nashville is a surprising town. You expect a sleepy little down-South scene but it's a whole other bag.

First of all, on the trip in from the airport, we figured we were in a city of millionaires. Eddie and I had never seen so many big rambling houses with so much lawn around them.

Second, when we got where we were going, it turned out a lot different from what we expected. The street corner sign said "16th Avenue South." But to most cats in the business, the street is known as "Music Street."

It was about eight-thirty when we hit the corner of 16th and Hillsboro. What I expected to see—if there was anything to see at this early hour—was a bunch of hillbilly hayseed types hanging around in blue overalls and red bandanas, humming on kazoos and moaning into harmonicas.

What I saw instead was kind of an eyeopener.

I mean, I'm a big-city boy. Chicago couldn't surprise me and neither can New York any more. Outside of them and Los Angeles, maybe, I used to figure the country was full of nothing.

But Music Street is something else, baby, let me tell you. First of all, the music part of it is only a few blocks. Then it shades off into a regular neighborhood where people live. Lots of trees line the street. But they do all over Nashville.

In those few blocks of Music Street, just about every big record company in the country has offices. And not just offices—studios. I mean they cut platters in Nashville.

And not just the country and western platters. Plenty of big rock people come down to Nashville to record, cats like Bob Dylan and the rest.

The reason is what they call the "Nashville Sound." It's hard to describe. Some people call it "white soul," but that doesn't tell you much.

The same way black soul music sounds—you know, exactly right for what it is—that's how the Nashville sound sounds.

Okay, I'll try again.

Say you dig somebody like Ray Charles, who is Mr. Soul among the Negro singers. Every note is right. Every sound works. The beat is what the beat should be. "Soul" is the black man's own music, at ease with itself, doing its own thing and not copying from anybody.

The Nashville sound is country people doing their own thing. It's different from black music, but just as honest to what it's supposed to be.

Well, none of that went through my mind when we hit Music Street that morning. What I was thinking was a lot different.

I was thinking we were on a wild goose chase. The waitress at the airport was cute and friendly. But what did she know about anything?

Anyway, we stood on the corner for a while. There wasn't any sign of life from any of the buildings where the big record companies were. Down the block on the left-hand side was this giant glass-front building. It was a museum of country and western music.

Eddie and I stood in front of the window and looked inside for a while. They had all kinds of stuff in there. You had to dig country music to dig the stuff. You know, a banjo played by somebody famous. That sort of thing.

We got tired of staring inside, so we walked over to the office building the waitress had sent us to. It was about three stories high. In the lobby downstairs the names of maybe fifty companies were listed.

We couldn't figure out how so many companies could be in one small office building. Then Eddie pointed out that the list showed a dozen companies listed under one room number.

We were looking for a cat named Colonel Crumpacker.

The waitress had written his name in full: Col. Aloysius "Zez" Crumpacker. I figured the "Zez" was a nickname, like from Aloysi-zez. The Crumpacker was a stopper, though.

According to the list in the lobby, Colonel Crumpacker hung his hat in room 309. So did about five other companies, all of them with names like "Talent-Boosters of America" or "Demo-Disk, International."

We hadn't seen anybody go in the building yet. But we decided to climb up to the third floor and park outside room 309.

Once we got upstairs, though, we realized something was happening inside 309. Some of the worst sounds I've ever heard were coming through the glass door.

We opened the door and stepped inside. It was an awfully big room. More than half of it was a sound studio with a big triple-plate-glass panel. Through the glass we could see instruments and mikes.

The other half of the room was filing cabinets and one desk. At the desk sat a man about the size of a ten-year-old boy. What I mean is, he was probably about five feet tall. And with the four-inch cowboy boots he was wearing, he figured to come about up to my chin.

The music—if that's what it was—was coming from a big audio panel on the wall. The short-portion gent was spinning a little 45 rpm. disk and what came out of the speakers was horrible.

"Oh, Mommah-baby, woncha baby-baby Mommah for me?" a voice was crying. Behind it about the worst rock combo in the entire world was laying down the usual idiot four-four beat.

"Colonel Crumpacker?" I asked.

He didn't turn around. He didn't even know we were in the room. With that noise, he probably didn't know he was still on Earth.

"Colonel Crumpacker?" I shouted.

He snapped a switch and sweet peace filled the room. Then he jumped to his feet. Sure enough, he reached my chin. "What's cooking, son?" he snapped.

He must've been in his sixties, and left out to dry in the sun most of that time. He had longish white hair, longish white sideburns and the world's longest white moustache.

"A chick told us to see you," I said. "She figured what you needed most in life was another guitah pickah. That's Eddie. And a piano man. That's me."

His little blue eyes narrowed down to tiny specks. "You union?"

I got the message at once. This gentleman wanted to pay on the cheap. I started to say yes and go chase yourself. But Eddie popped in again.

"Just in Chicago," he said.

Colonel Crumpacker's eyes relaxed a silly millimeter or two. "Zat so," he rumbled. "Hum."

"Hum," I said. "What kind of work you got going?"

"Hum," said he. "I got a hundred a week in cash, no questions asked, for two lads who can read and fake."

"Hum," I said. "That's a hundred apiece."

"Hum, no," the Colonel admitted.

"So long, suh," I said.

I grabbed Eddie and started to get us out of there. "Easy, boy," the Colonel called after us. "It never does to rush in this climate. Let me hear a few bars of something."

I kept on walking, but Eddie hung back. He put

74

his guitar case on a chair, flipped it open and brought out the demo tape. "Here," he said.

"Where?" I asked, short-stopping the tape and dropping it in my pocket. "That's top-secret stuff, Eddie."

Colonel Crumpacker's eyes widened like a cat's in a dark room. His milky blue irises looked very shiny.

"My problem," I told the good Colonel, "is that I'm not as wild as my buddy here. Before I get going, like I have to know what business you're in, Colonel, suh."

He spread his arms out wide and his moustaches fluttered like the wings of a proud bird. "Son, my life is an open book," he stated. "I am what you call a public benefactor. I do good for others."

"Beautiful," I said.

"People with talent come to me," the Colonel told us. "They write in from all over the country. Little people. Poor people. But people with great talent, yearning to break free."

"You help them make the break."

"Exactly, son." His eyes beamed blindingly upon me. "If someone has the idea for a song, we write it up for him. We make a demo record and send the record all over the country. Disk jockeys from coast to coast hear the record. They play it on the air. In no time at all, the composer becomes a millionaire."

I nodded. "Gotcha. And you need house musicians to play for the demo recording."

75

It was the Colonel's turn to nod. "For which I will pay you boys the princely stipend of one hundred and fifty a week."

"Each?"

"Hum."

I took Eddie's arm. "Come on, Eddie. Let's go."

"Hold it again, son," Colonel Crumpacker called. "You are the hastiest young man I have ever run into."

I should say that the Colonel's accent was about as wide as a football field. What he said was "Ye-ew aw th'hastiest young may-an Ah hay-ave evuh run in-tuh." But who can read it that way?

I stopped and turned back to him. "Can I ask you a couple of questions?"

"Fire away, son."

"Is it because you pay so low that you are always looking to pick up a few musicians? Is that why the waitress at the airport gave us your name?"

The Colonel tilted his head sideways, like a bird looking at a worm. "That's a leading question, son. I decline to answer."

"Second question," I said. "If somebody sends you a song to record, how much do they pay you?"

Colonel Crumpacker smiled slightly. "A personal question, son. I do not choose to respond."

"Third. I've heard about outfits like yours. Isn't it true that if you record somebody's song, they sign over half-ownership to you?"

76

"I do not care to dignify that question with an answer, son."

I sighed. "Okay. Three strikes are out. Come on, Eddie, let's blow."

"Boys," the Colonel said, "you keep right on asking questions. How else are you ever going to learn anything?"

So that started us laughing a little. Pretty soon he was offering a hundred bucks a week for each of us.

"But we won't be here more than a few weeks," I warned him. "We're on our way to New York."

He nodded slowly, like a little white-haired old owl.

"They all are, son. They all are."

17

At first we thought we'd cool off in Nashville about a week or two at the most. I sent a note to Carol, telling her what'd happened. I said she should wait till she heard from me in New York.

Wait for what, I don't know. She and I didn't really have anything going, did we? I tried to figure that one out, but I didn't get anywhere with it.

Eddie lectured me a little. "You stuck up for her.

You maybe saved her life," he said. "So there's a thing between you."

"You're freaked out, man."

"I'm serious, Stosh. If you save somebody's life, you got like a—a duty to them."

"Crazy."

He shrugged. "Even if that isn't so, you know you had eyes for her from the start."

"Yeah," I admitted. "She's easy to watch. But what do I want to keep mailing her my address for?"

Eddie didn't have any answer to that. So I kept on going. "It'd be different if, say, she was a singer. Like, maybe we'd cut a number with her handling the vocal."

Eddie gave me a pained look. "The wild stuff you write? No chick is goofed enough to sing your songs."

"Or, maybe if she had some other angle to her. Like, man, she was the greatest sex-bomb east of the Mississippi or something."

Eddie shook his head sadly. "You got some idea of what's good about chicks. With that Frankie you nearly ended up under a stone."

I gave him a how-could-any-one-cat-get-so-dumb look. "I never knew how great an expert on chicks you were, Eddie."

He blushed. "That's not the thing. The thing is you know even less than I do."

"So how come we're not discussing one of your chicks?"

This turned him off completely. I waited to hear from him again and when he stayed turned off, I picked up again.

"Just because I tried to help some broad doesn't mean I'm serious about her."

"We're on the lam from the mob. How much more serious do you want it?"

I looked at Eddie. He looked at me. "I'm not even sure the mob is looking for us," I said.

"That's why we're holed up in Nashville, playing rotten songs for a con-man promoter? Because the mob doesn't want us?"

I stopped looking at Eddie. He stopped looking at me.

18

□ □ □ □ □ □ □ □ □ □ □ □ □ □

I'll say one thing about Nashville. Time passes quickly.

Christmas came and went. I got a card from Carol. I sent her a card. Eddie sent his folks a card. They sent him one. I'm pretty sure they could have told my folks where I was. But—

It wasn't the world's greatest Christmas. But time really passed.

I mean, what with the countryside and the great food and the friendly people, it was four weeks before I woke up and remembered that we still weren't in New York.

I had worked out a separate job for myself, moonlighting nights in a little bar and grill. It was on a street in Nashville called Printer's Alley.

Printer's Alley is an alley, all right. I mean a real, honest alley down in the business district of town. What it's got to do with printers I never found out.

But it's the street all those tired tigers go to late at night after the convention or the meeting's over. My job lasted from about dinner-time till about one in the morning. I was relief pianist for a cool one-fifty a week.

You dig? Between us, Eddie and I were pulling in three-fifty a week. We never had it so good.

At this Printer's Alley joint I would fill in between the regular floor show. I'd get up here in a rented tux and give the people the golden oldies.

About one A.M. I'd get back to the fleabag room Eddie and I had in a motel near Music Street. He'd be asleep already. I'd hit the sack.

The telephone would go off at seven-thirty A.M. to let us know we had an hour to get washed, dressed and down to Colonel Crumpacker's do-good establishment.

What a racket he had. What a con. He took little

ads in all the confession magazines, the movie fan mags, the men's girlie mags. You know.

"Make the most of your talent! You always suspected you could write songs as good as those you hear on the air! Now find out! Have your tune orchestrated and performed by top professional musicians in the music capital of the world—Nashville! Hear your number performed on a genuine 'demo' record you can play on your own phonograph for friends and at parties! Earn big money! Small processing charge leads to big profits!"

Then he would put in the name of one of his five different companies, with an address to write to.

I'll say one thing for the Colonel's swindle. It was more or less honest. Aside from the blarney he gave them in the ads, his suckers got their money's worth.

At least when Eddie and I were there, they did. We would get these songs any old way. Some of the suckers had scribbled them down on paper. Some had hummed them into their home tape recorder.

Whatever way we got them, Eddie and I and a drummer named George Whitefeather had about ten minutes to figure it out. Then the Colonel would tell us which one was to sing the song and off we went, tape turning and mike open.

If we took longer than fifteen minutes to arrange and record a song, Colonel Crumpacker began to get awful nervous.

"Speed, boys," he'd tell us. He worked as his own engineer. "Speed means money in this business."

"I thought we were just doing good, not making money," I told him.

"Here's your next song. Get going, boys."

Incidentally, I guess the name George White-feather rings a bell. He's still drummer for the Flesh-Colored Bandaid. George is half Cherokee and half about five other things. In those days he didn't even belong to the union.

That's why the Colonel hired him. Eddie and I were asking for trouble by working for a non-union employer. If the union ever found out we'd be in a real box.

And the union already knew I was there because the job on Printer's Alley was a union gig for scale.

"Far as I can see," George told me one afternoon at the Colonel's studio, "belonging to the union is more trouble than it's worth."

"You're wrong. But I won't argue with you. Why don't you join up?"

"Not me. I get my fifty a week steady from the Colonel. I'm happy."

I was kind of shocked. This was the first I knew George was so badly underpaid. "You'd earn three times that if this were a union gig," I told him.

"But it ain't," he said. "So?"

So he had me there. For the time being. We were sitting around having a smoke about four in the afternoon. The Colonel was away for an hour. We sure didn't intend to do any work while he wasn't there.

It had been a busy day. The Colonel hadn't even had time to open his mail from the morning. It was spilled out all over his desk. I lifted up one envelope and held it to the light.

Inside I could see somebody had clipped the Colonel's ad from a magazine. There was a five-dollar bill with the ad.

Of the thirty or so letters and cards on the desk, I figured most had money in them, with more loot to come. It cost you a cool fifty clams if you wanted the Colonel to send you a demo disk. The fiver was just a deposit to make sure you didn't back out.

I picked up another piece of mail, a postcard. It was from a radio station out in Glendale, California.

The Colonel sent these cards out with every demo disk to the jockeys. If you wanted that service from the Colonel, it cost you an arm and a leg over the original fifty.

This postcard was what they call a "use" card. It was already typed up for the disk jockey to fill out in pen or pencil. It had spaces for the call letters of the station and the jock's name. It had little squares he was supposed to check yes or no.

If he filled it out right, the Colonel could tell if the jock had played a particular demo or not and, if so, how many times.

Then the Colonel would report this to the composer of the song and sandbag him for a few more bucks.

As I said, it was a con, but it was sort of a fair one.

The swindle part of it was that the Colonel never told any of his suckers if the song was worth promoting. Rotten or not, the Colonel acted as if it were the greatest song ever written.

I looked at a few more use cards that disk jockeys had mailed back to the Colonel. "He must send out hundreds of demos," I said.

George pulled open a file cabinet and showed me a whole stack of cards with names and addresses on them. "There must be three or four hundred names."

"Say," I said. "I just got an—"

The telephone rang and I answered it. It was the Colonel, telling us he wouldn't be back and for us to lock the door on our way out.

Which was all I needed to know.

1⑨

![decorative filmstrip divider]

I don't know if I ever told you I was kind of handy with electrical stuff. For instance, the wired-up ruby I wore on my head. The one with the flashing lights in it? I rigged that myself.

I guess I've been fooling around with tape record-
ers and electric pianos and amplifiers and such since
I was maybe twelve years old.

Anyway, the set-up in the Colonel's studio was
simple. Even the Colonel could work it. He would
cut a tape of each number we played. Then he would
re-record the first half-minute or so on another tape.

He would send this tiny bit of tape to the sucker.
It was a real come-on. The letter with it said:

"Dear Composer: play this tape clip on your recorder and hear, for the first time, how your very
own song sounds as arranged and performed by top
professional Nashville musicians."

The rest of the letter would tell the chump that if
he wanted the whole tape and a demo disk, it would
now cost him the rest of the fifty bucks.

If the sucker kicked in the loot, the Colonel would
re-record the tape on a small cutting turntable. It
made a pretty decent vinyl 45 rpm. platter. It wasn't
top quality, but okay as a demo.

I think only about ten out of every ten suckers
kicked in the extra loot. How could they refuse? It
was cheap enough to hear their brainchild performed by us genuine Nashville cats.

I had been watching the Colonel at work for the
last few weeks. Once in a while he got a real live one,
a sucker who wanted his demo sent around the country to disk jockeys.

The Colonel would send the tape to a recording

lab. They would turn out three hundred demos with the label of the Colonel's own publishing company on it. (I had been right. The chumps gave him a half-interest in the song. It was part of the contract they signed.)

That afternoon, George Whitefeather left the studio around five. Eddie and I sat there till eight, copying the disk jockey names onto three hundred envelopes the size of a 45 rpm. disk.

We took all the envelopes home. Next day, when the Colonel went out for lunch, I sent our own demo tape from Chicago to the recording lab. I used one of the Colonel's blanks. But I wrote on it:

"Do not use labels on disks. Return disks without labels."

While we were waiting for the three hundred demos to come back, I found two copyright forms the Colonel had lying around. Eddie and I filled out a form for "Dead Abe" and one for "King of Things."

We took the forms to a notary public in a little stationery store down 16th Street. He knew all about copyright forms.

We got money orders and sent the forms to Washington, D.C. Now, no matter what happened, "Dead Abe" and "King of Things" belonged to us and nobody else. They would be copyrighted with the U.S. Government.

The day the demo disks came back, the Colonel

nearly caught wise to what we were doing. But I latched onto them before he got too curious.

That night Eddie and I took home the demos and three hundred use cards. While I was at work in Printer's Alley, Eddie stuffed three hundred envelopes. He licked three hundred stamps and mailed out the demos. He saved a dozen disks for later on if we needed them.

The plan was gorgeous. It couldn't fail.

I figured we were swindling the Colonel a little, but we were going to give him a chance at the action later. So I didn't feel too bad about it.

When the use cards came back—if the disk was a hit—he'd wonder who wrote "Dead Abe" and "King of Things." We wouldn't tell him.

He'd go off his rocker trying to figure out which sucker had produced a hit song, right? But we'd just let him sweat.

Finally, if the song really caught on, we'd let him know who owned the copyright. Then we'd let him handle the action for an agent's ten per cent. But not for the 50 per cent he was used to getting as a half-owner.

Beautiful plan, right?

Wrong.

20

It was a Thursday night. I remember it very well because there weren't too many people around the joint on Printer's Alley.

Eddie and I had been in Nashville almost six weeks. The demo disks had been mailed out about two weeks before.

It was about, say, quarter to midnight. There were a few younger couples listening to me. I was wandering through an old Gershwin number called "How Long Has This Been Going On?"

I was working out a chorus or two in spread-out style. You know, the bass notes are way down near the bottom of the keyboard. The melody is up so high you wouldn't know the tune if you didn't already know. Dig?

Mr. Muscles walked in the front door, my old boss from Chicago. He didn't look around, the way they do in the movies. He already knew just where to look. Right at the piano.

Another guy had come in with him, a guy even taller and heftier. Both of them trench coats with the belts hanging down at the side.

The other guy started circling the room. I could see he was moving toward the kitchen door the waiters used. He figured to cut me off if I made a break for it.

I could see Muscles heading straight for me, not fast and not slow either. I could see all kinds of things. I could see that I shouldn't have taken a union job because it's very easy to check the union and ask them where one of their members is playing.

As he passed the bar, Muscles picked up a chromium-plated stool and took it along with him as if it were a toothpick.

So far, nobody had noticed anything. Or if they had, they weren't saying much about it. The headwaiter was talking to the bartender. The checkroom chick was talking to the boss. The customers were talking to each other. And I was knocking out "How Long Has This Been Going On?"

Muscles was about fifteen feet from me now. He was smiling at me in a funny way, all teeth and nostrils. He looked about nine feet tall. The barstool looked even taller.

I reached sideways for the piano mike. I shoved it up against the bandstand loudspeaker. Then I turned the amplifier volume up full.

The feedback howled through the room like an express train. The scream went up until it began to split eardrums. Everybody jumped and stared at me.

I backed through the curtains behind the bandstand. Muscles began to dive for me. His buddy started after him.

I ducked behind the curtains and made it into the washroom the waiters use. I locked the door. The room was tiny, with a window about at the level of my face.

Muscles figured out where I was. I heard the stool smash against the washroom door. It boomed like a drum. The door shook. A hinge popped.

I slid open the window and started to scramble up into it. I heard a loud crash behind me. I heard splintering.

I turned back to look for half a second. Muscles threw the barstool at me. I ducked. The stool slammed into my left shoulder. I flew out the window like a cork out of a bottle.

I think my legs were working even before I hit the pavement. I started running down a little garbage lane, into an alley and into another one.

I could hear shouting behind me and footsteps. I turned another corner. Muscles saw me and yelped. I turned and ran.

Down another alley I found a Mustang convertible parked next to some garbage cans. Whoever owned it was awful trusting. They'd left the keys in it.

I jumped in, started the car and roared off down another alley. Muscles' friend showed up in front of me. I gave him the horn and he ducked into a doorway to keep from being run down.

Ten minutes later I'd stashed the heap behind our motel. I woke Eddie. It took us five minutes to pack and blow. I started cruising Nashville, wondering what to do next. Muscles had to find me sometime, somewhere. But I wasn't going to let it be now and here.

We checked the airport from a pay phone and found that there was a flight to New York in forty minutes. I gunned the Mustang and we made it out there in half an hour. But Muscles' friend was already there. I could see him pacing up and down near the ticket counters.

I headed the Mustang back into Nashville and parked around the corner from the train depot. This was some building. In the moonlight it looked like one of these ancient cathedrals, full of knobs and windows and spires and all that.

There was an eastbound train for Philadelphia and Baltimore due through the depot in an hour.

I left Eddie in a telephone booth at the train station. His orders were to keep his eyes open. Muscles might not spot him as easily as he'd spot me.

I drove around a while trying to figure my next move. If we didn't show at the airport, Muscles and friend might get tired of lying in wait and try something else. The train depot was a natural place to look. So was the bus depot.

I stopped at a pay phone and called the police. I said I was calling for the manager of the joint in Printer's Alley. I reported an attempted assault and gave them good descriptions of Muscles and his buddy. I said I thought they'd lam out by plane or train or bus.

The cop sounded kind of sarcastic as he said, "Thanks for telling us our business," and hung up.

Then I took the car back to Printer's Alley, careful to come in from the opposite direction. I left the car about where I remembered picking it up. Then I walked back to the train depot.

Whatever else happened, at least they couldn't pin a car-theft rap on me. I had enough troubles without that.

I got to the station about the time a squad-car pulled up. Two cops made a quick check of the people waiting in the depot and left.

I rousted Eddie from the telephone booth. We sneaked out along the track where the eastbound train was due to come in.

When it did, we got on without buying tickets. I figured we could pay the conductor when he came around. It was better than being caught at the ticket window.

We found a seat in a coach car. The lights were turned very low. All around us people were trying to sleep. Across the aisle a woman had a baby on her lap. She was humming in its ear and trying to get it to drink a bottle of milk.

I watched her for a while. The train pulled out of Nashville. I watched the aisle, looking for Muscles. Nobody showed but the conductor.

I listened to the woman humming to her baby. Pretty soon I was fast asleep.

21

Oh, sure, we finally got to New York.

Let me tell you about the day we got there, okay?

In summer, New York is too darned hot. Whatever the temperature is, it feels twice as hot. The air conditioners pump heat out onto the street. The water in the air melts your collar. But summer is heaven compared to winter in New York.

And, baby, it was winter when we hit New York. We made our grand entrance early in February on a Greyhound bus from Philly.

It had been snowing. The streets were full of a kind of brown-gray mush that got over your shoe uppers. Your feet were wet in one minute and freezing a minute later.

A wind blew across town. Not even the tall buildings could break its force. It came at your eyes like claws. Pretty soon you couldn't see from the tears. Then it would grab at your cheeks.

You'd stand in a doorway to get away from the wind. Specks of dirt and cinders would fall down on you. The ones that didn't fall on you went into your lungs when you took a breath.

Nobody looked at you. Nobody looked up from the slush on the street. Armies of people kept walking in every direction, heads down into the wind. No matter where you were walking, you were just marching along in a platoon with fifty other people.

If you were coming to a corner and the light turned green, you tried to cross the street. But there were so many people, you'd only fight halfway across and the light would turn red.

You were always bumping into people and they into you. If it was a man, he'd say something you couldn't really hear and walk away. If it was a woman, she'd glare at you and spit out a word like "Filth!" and look for a cop.

That was our first day in town. We wandered around near the bus depot till we hit the upper end of Times Square. Then we wandered around looking at the shops.

They sold all sorts of high-class stuff, cheapie radios and cameras, dirty books, kewpie dolls, hats with your name on them, buttons with cursewords, posters that made fun of important people and hot dogs.

This was the Big Time, all right.

We found a hotel on a sidestreet in the Forties off Times Square. For ten bucks a day we could share a double bed, no radio, no TV, no air conditioning. It was double what we paid in Nashville, but it was the Big Time. The clerk at the hotel said we wouldn't find any place cheaper in town. He was right.

We put our shoes on the radiator to dry out. Then I started talking. It was such a bad scene that I didn't trust myself to think quietly. I had to talk.

"Things could be worse," I started telling Eddie.

"You sure?"

"Much worse. We still have our demo tape. And we've got a lot more money than when we left Chicago. I figure we could stay in New York two months on what we have."

"I have a better idea," Eddie said. "I'll go home to Chicago. That way you can stay here four months. And you're welcome to it." He got up and went to the window.

"Eddie, how can you say that? This is the Big Time. This is where we make it, baby."

"That's the Big Time, huh?" He jerked his head at the street outside the window. I looked out. Traffic was tied up as far as I could see in each direction.

Every time the corner light turned green, the cars

would honk and hoot and make a racket. They would move forward a few yards and then the light would turn red.

"I see what you mean," I said, and sat down on the edge of the bed. "Still and all, there is only one New York, Eddie."

"And it's all yours."

"You'll get used to it. We knew it wouldn't be easy to crack, baby. But we can't quit the day we get here."

"Is there a law that says we can't?" Eddie asked. "Because, if there is, I'm breaking it."

I made a face. I didn't feel too much different. But, after all, Muscles wasn't after Eddie. He could go back to Chicago and probably get away with it.

"Okay," I said.

"Huh?"

"Tomorrow morning, you hit the road for Chicago."

He looked at me for a while. "Alone?"

"I can't go back. Muscles wouldn't just beat me up. After Nashville he'd kill me."

He kept on looking at me. "What will you do then?"

"Gig around New York. There have to be jobs."

"He'll track you down through the union."

"I'll work non-union."

"You'll starve," Eddie said. "Okay, I'm staying."

"What?"

He sat down on the other side of the bed. "I'm staying. If you're alone here, trying to earn a buck while you peddle the demo, you'll never do either one."

"I'll make out."

"Nuts." Eddie got up and went to the radiator. "The shoes are almost dry. How about we go out and get some dinner?"

So the two of us spent our first night in New York at a hot-dog counter. I had three and Eddie had two. With mustard.

22

The weather never did get any better that month. We found out the town was cold and nasty and miserable to strangers. But after a while, we made a few friends and we weren't strangers.

I wrote Carol and gave her my new address. Don't ask me why.

I had almost forgotten what she looked like. The second week in New York, I found a job for Eddie and me. It was in a little off-off-Broadway theatre down in Greenwich Village.

This part of town has to be seen to be believed. It's

very old. Some of the buildings go back to Colonial days. And it's full of characters, hippies and junkies and artists and musicians and actors. Especially actors.

We were hired as the pit band for a show. This is sort of funny if you know that a Broadway pit band can have fifty guys in it. But off-off-Broadway sometimes the whole band is just a piano. So you can see that a piano and a guitar is Big Time, right?

This show was a revue. It had songs and skits. Except for a few minutes when a skit was on, Eddie and I played all the time. We rehearsed from right after lunch every day until midnight every night. The dancers were collapsing. The singers were hoarse. The actors fell asleep on their feet. And for this we each got twenty-five clams a week.

Big Time.

The director of the show was also the writer. He was a little guy about twenty-five years old with long sideburns and hair down over his collar. Wherever he went a lady of about fifty went with him.

She had shorter hair than he did and she wore a skirt shorter than any of the nineteen-year-old dancers in the revue. She was about my mother's age, but she still saw herself as a swinger. I figured she was the director's mother. But it turned out she was the producer.

"Producer?" I asked one of the singers, a chick named Yvonne.

"Yeah, she puts up the money for the show."
Yvonne had bright red hair and big blue eyes. She
lived by herself a few blocks from the theatre.

"Why would anybody spend money on this show?"
I asked her.

She had invited me to her pad for dinner and we
were lying around afterwards listening to some kind
of new classical music from her phonograph. It
sounded way out, electronic stuff, a real gas.

"Because she's the director's girlfriend," Yvonne
said.

We lit up a pair of joints. The stuff was mellow. I
hadn't had any grass since Frankie. The first joint
did nothing for me. But the second one grabbed.

"Why couldn't she be the girlfriend of somebody
who wrote a good show?"

We were lying on a heavy rug on the floor. The air
was thick with that real pot stink. We started kissing.

23

Next week Eddie and I moved into a rooming
house down in the village. We paid twenty-five a
week—a week's salary—for a room. We shared the
bath with three other guys. But it was in the same

block with the theatre where we were rehearsing.

Mornings he and I would make the rounds of agents. We saw music publishers and other people who might help us. We'd try to get them to listen to the demo. But all they'd do is take the platter and promise to let us know. Sometimes they wouldn't even take the platter.

Eddie was getting more and more fed up. He was sure these people never played the demos. He felt they just threw the platters in the wastebasket the minute we were out the door.

Also, he was mad at me because I was back on grass.

"Be happy it's just grass, baby," I told him one day at rehearsal. "The kind of cats in this show, we could make any scene at all. Speed, acid, even H and M."

He nodded and his face looked unhappy. "That's your next scene, man," he said. "This Yvonne is bad news. So are her friends."

"She's no user."

"Can you say that for the friends?"

He had me there, so I dropped the subject.

As I kept trying to tell Eddie, we were in great shape. Thanks to the jobs, we were making our nest egg last longer. And he couldn't make me believe that the music people were throwing away our demos without playing them.

"Why should they play them?" Eddie asked. "They must get a dozen demos a day chucked at their heads. From people they know and respect. Why listen to some guys who come in off the street?"

A funny thing happened about that time. I didn't think too much of it. When you're on grass, baby, little details just zip right by you. You're never sure where you heard something or who said it. Or if you just dreamed it.

I mean, I wasn't on a permanent high. But every night after rehearsal, this Yvonne chick and I would really climb out of sight. She'd turn her record player on. We'd play that groovy classical stuff. Or she'd switch to FM radio and we'd dig a concert.

One morning about two A.M. I was falling asleep. I could hear Yvonne in the little kitchenette, putting some ice cubes in a glass and running the cold water.

She was humming something. I couldn't quite place the tune, but it was one I knew. It sounded sort of weird, but friendly.

"What's that?" I asked her.

She took her time coming back into the room. "What's what?"

But by then I was out of sight again.

The days went by that way. It's funny how pot shortens up everything. I mean, while you're high, everything seems to move slowly. But if you add up the days into weeks, they shoot right past.

One night Yvonne took me to a party after rehearsal. Half the people there were up-heads and the other half were down-heads. You dig a scene like that? Up-heads are on speed or some kind of meth. Down-heads go for the sleepy-time pills. It was like being at two different parties.

My scene wasn't up or down. So, like, I was digging the best of both scenes. I happened to be talking to a down chick, real stop-time mamma. She had the lowest, slowest voice I ever heard.

I was trying to put her words together. You know, they came so slowly you kind of forgot one before the next one showed up. Across the room was this cat my age, a musician.

How did I know? Well, he was wearing tattersall slacks ripped off about two inches over the ankle. A gold chain was his belt. He had a silver chain wound around his head. That was it. No shirt, no shoes, but he was carrying a guitar case.

That's how I knew he was a musician.

That's how square I was to the New York scene. I thought a cat who carried around a guitar case was a musician. I saw a guy walking the streets with a white plastic motorcyclist's helmet hanging from his hand. He had goggles in his other hand. I thought he owned a motorbike, right?

Or I saw one cat walking around the Village carrying one of those big round flat cans that movie film comes in. I thought he made movies, right?

Wrong. New York is full of very talented phonies. I mean their talent is for being phony. They think they can make it better with the chicks if they come on as something groovy like a musician or a film-maker or a cat with a bike.

Anyway, this Shoeless Joe was whistling a little tune I dug. Man, it was a gas. I stopped listening to the down-head chick and started across the room to Mr. Speed.

"Hey, man, like, you know," I said getting revved up to ask him a question.

He turned on me as if I was carrying a knife. His eyes were wide and showing a lot of white, like a real meth-head. His teeth were chattering. Maybe it was because he had no shirt.

"Back off, Jack," he muttered. "Stop climbing me."

Up-heads get that way, very suspicious. I stepped back from Benzedrine Charley. "What's that tune you were whistling?" I asked him.

He frowned at me. "What tune?"

So I kind of drifted off to find Yvonne.

24

All this time, of course, Eddie and I were trying to batter down the doors of the music business. Only the music business was battering us down instead.

That whole New York scene was too much, man. I mean, we didn't really dig the rules. We couldn't even tell the players. And nobody gave us a score-card.

Like, right off the bat, I knew nobody in New York was going to dig our sound. They were all on another sound that year, raga-rock.

You probably don't remember that year any more, or raga-rock, either. It was from Indian music. It used stringed instruments like the sitar. And it kind of droned on and on and never seemed to go any-where.

It was nice to listen to. It made you feel kind of dreamy. But the second you put words to it, you had a guaranteed dog. Nobody could sing raga-rock and make it mean anything.

But in New York that year, raga-rock was The Thing. Plus electronic tricks.

I told you I'm not bad on the electronics thing my-self. I know a few dozen ways to put sounds through electronic gizmos. I can make them come out all shook up and groovy.

But that year in New York they were doing things with electronics that would make a math teacher scratch his head. For instance, in the recording stu-dios, they had two mikes for each player.

One mike would pick up the sound straight and take it right to the control board. The other mike would take the sound of the same instrument and

104

shove it through echo chambers and delay-lines and reverb circuits and vibrato or tremolo filters.

What came out you wouldn't believe.

And in the control booth, the engineers would play with the channels from the instruments. On one chorus they'd bring up the bass guitar so full it sounded like an orchestra. On another, they blank out the whole track except a thin treble range. It made a sound like a guy strangling to death in a shower stall.

Then they would try other tricks. Like, you know, recording one man at a time. First the drummer would do the whole number by himself on tape. Then they'd play back the tape through headphones. The guitar would listen to the drum on headphones while he recorded his own tape in time to the drum.

They'd keep adding instruments and playing with the sound and mixing one tape with another. That year in New York they didn't care what they did to music.

So when we came along with our samba-rock sound, no tricks, just music, they must've thought they had the squares of all time on their hands.

In other words, man, they didn't dig Eddie and me at all.

So we kept on playing for rehearsals of this show. The director kept firing people and hiring new people. He kept throwing out songs and putting in new ones.

By then, he'd fired Yvonne, too. I started seeing another chick in the show, a dancer.

"You already have a dancer on the string," Eddie told me. He was trying to make me feel ashamed of something.

"Who?"

"Carol is who."

"Miss Ottumwa, Iowa?" I asked. "She doesn't even know I'm alive."

Which shows you how smart I was.

25

Finally, opening night.

Everybody was pretty excited. The critics had been invited down to review the show. Everybody's friends had free tickets. The director and his lady friend were so keyed up they were walking about a foot off the ground.

I had always thought the show was rotten. But I wasn't ready for the reviews the next morning.

"Somebody goofed," the critic wrote. "It was the man who put in the exit doors. There should have been an exit next to every seat in the theatre. As it was, I spent five minutes trying to get out and had to listen to five minutes more of the worst show ever written, directed, acted, sung, danced, played or produced."

I got the feeling he was trying to tell us something. The afternoon paper's critic was much kinder. "This play has a great future. It should be sold to the U.S. Army. Let any enemy try to attack us and we will show him a scene from this play—any scene—and watch him drop dead in his tracks."

So, that evening, when we came to the theatre, the door was locked. A few of the actors were standing around outside.

It turned out that nobody could locate the director or his lady friend. He skipped out owing us all a week's salary.

Eddie and I went home to our furnished room. We counted the money we had left. For nearly a month, we had been trying to score in New York. We had enough money left for about one more month.

"But you can't tell me," Eddie said, "that in the next month something good is going to happen."

It didn't. Not only was no one interested in our demo, but neither of us could find another job. To make it worse, we had one of those March blizzards for which New York is famous.

Instead of slush around our ankles, we had it around our knees. We had stopped eating in restaurants and cafeterias. We had even stopped eating at hot-dog stands.

107

That's right, we were heating cans of chili on an electric iron. It wasn't bad. Sometimes I would switch to a can of spaghetti. With meatballs.

I remember the day our money ran out. It was April First, April Fool's Day. We owed two weeks' rent and we had just come back from making the rounds. Our landlady had locked us out.

This is a feeling I don't wish on anybody. All your clothes are in your room. You may not own much, but whatever it is, you can't get at it. Not till you pay your rent.

So we cleared away some of the slush from the front steps of the rooming house and sat down. We tried to figure out what to do next.

"We could get some money by hocking our clothes," Eddie suggested.

"If we could get to our clothes."

"Yeah, I forgot." He thought for a while. "I could hock my guitar if. . . ." He sighed. "If I could get to my guitar."

A big oil truck came tearing down the street, trying to make the green light at the corner. The truck's tires hit a pot hole in the pavement. A big wave of dirty brown slush shot into the air. It fell on top of us.

I don't know which of us got the worst of it. We turned to look at each other. I brushed some slush off Eddie's nose. He brushed some off my shoulder.

108

We sat there and felt the slush sinking into our clothes. Beautiful.

"You look awful," Carol said.

It was her, all right. She was standing on the sidewalk looking up at us on the steps. And beside her stood Colonel Aloysius "Zez" Crumpacker.

26

Well, the rest of it you've probably read in the fan magazines.

That tune I had heard Yvonne sing. It was the one the meth-head had whistled. But I was too deep in grass to know it.

The tune was "Dead Abe."

Can you figure it? The tune I wrote and sweated over and was starving to death in New York to plug. I was so dopey on pot I didn't even know it was my own music.

Worse, I didn't even wonder how they had heard of "Dead Abe."

You remember the demos we sent out to disk jockeys? The ones the Colonel didn't know about? The ones without labels.

Some of the jocks dug the tunes. They liked "Dead Abe" and they creamed over "King of Things." But there was a mystery about the disk. Some of them played the numbers but there wasn't much they could tell their fans.

A jockey in San Francisco played the platter twice a night for a month. A guy in Chicago, one in Fort Worth, another in Omaha and one in Richmond— they all played it regularly.

Meanwhile, some of the jockeys tried to trace the disk back. They mailed in their use cards with little scribbled notes, "Man, who cut this disk? It's a groove," and stuff like that.

But Colonel Crumpacker had no idea. And George Whitefeather wasn't about to tell him because he was scared the Colonel would fire him when he found out.

Just when the Colonel was going out of his skull, the government sent back the copyright notice on the songs. So he knew right away Eddie and I had written the numbers and owned them.

That didn't help the Colonel. He had a hit on his hands. But until he got hold of us, he couldn't promote the record. He had no right to. He didn't own it.

So he started looking for us. He even put a private eye on the job. The eye dug up the story about my fight with Muscles in the Printer's Alley bar. That scared the Colonel quite a bit. He turned off the private eye.

He spent the next few weeks biting his nails while more and more use cards came in from disk jockeys saying "Great sound, daddy. Lay more on us."

Pity poor Colonel Crumpacker. For the first time in his life he was sitting on a hit platter. And there was nothing he could do. Or, rather, there was one thing he could do. So he did it.

He came to New York.

He figured we were dumb enough to be wasting away here trying to get a break. All he had to do was talk to one or two agents and music publishers. He found we had certainly been around, all right. Yes, one or two had played our disk. They hadn't dug it at all.

One agent told the colonel: "That 'Dead Abe' gives me the creeps." A publisher said: "I get junk like 'King of Things' every day of the week."

The colonel kept his yap shut about how the disk jockeys felt. You see, New York is where it's happening, baby, but the news hadn't hit town yet.

When I say you have to have luck in this business, I know what I'm talking about. The fan magazines say that I sent for Carol when we hit the big time. That's a lie.

She hadn't heard from me in months. She only had my old hotel address. When she hit town the hotel couldn't help her.

So she did just what Colonel Crumpacker did. She started asking agents and publishers. On her second day, she ran into the Colonel. They joined forces. On their fourth day of looking, they ran across an agent who remembered Eddie and I were working in a musical down in the Village.

Carol and the Colonel traced us to the theatre, but the door was still locked. So they had just about given up.

They saw the oil truck hit the pothole. They saw slush splash all over these two down-and-out creeps on the stairs of the rooming house.

And the rest is history.

27

I guess I'm lucky. Underneath that thief's chest of Colonel Crumpacker, there beat the heart of a true Southern gentleman.

After the dirty trick we played on him, he came through for us like a soldier. I guess the money he made on us helped him forget the dirty trick, huh?

Anyway, the first thing he did was set up a corporation for us. This was the Nova Company. Eddie and I were the president and secretary of it. There were no other officers. We owned all the stock, too.

Nova Company bought from us the rights to promote the two songs we owned. Nova also signed a contract with Colonel Aloysius Crumpacker to serve as exclusive agent for those two songs.

We sent for George Whitefeather. We sent out an audition call for a rhythm guitar and the best cat to show was Mo Manzo. I came up with the name Flesh-Colored Bandaid. We hired the best studio in New York and cut eight numbers, including "Dead Abe" and "King of Things."

Money? We were using the Colonel's money. Before he'd left Nashville, he'd drawn every cent he owned out of the bank. And he owned a few, too.

Now we got another inside view of the music business. We learned a rule, the one we didn't know before. The rule is very simple. It goes like this:

In the music business, when you're nobody, your music stinks. But when you're somebody, anything you play is a hit.

Why is that? I'm not sure. I only know that once the Flesh-Colored Bandaid got hot, there was no stopping us.

I suppose most of you remember—if you ever bothered to read about it—some of the things people said about "Dead Abe" and "King of Things."

They said "Dead Abe" was the sound of a disaster that had to be lived with. They said it was the sound of our time, violent, absurd and hypnotic.

How about that?

And they said "King of Things" was a cry from the

heart. It was a cry of despair. They said it put down the whole over-thirty generation for good.

Does that grab you?

I think the thing Eddie and I appreciated most was that people thought the two sides were "musicianly." I'm not sure what that means, but I think it meant to be nice.

Also, it sort of meant to be insulting to other pop music. I mean, like the other stuff wasn't done by musicians. But our stuff was.

I don't put the knock on any kind of music I don't dig. It would be like putting the knock on food I don't eat. It's all what you like, your own thing.

Plenty of pop music I know is played by sickies for sickies. And a lot of it is played by dopes for other dopes. But if that's what a person likes, if that's his scene, I don't knock it.

In the first six months after we got famous, people would try real hard to get us to put down other types of pop stuff.

First came our big 45 rpm. disk. This time it went out on a good label, one everyone knew. The record company promoted the grooves right off that platter. They sent it out in cartons by the five-hundreds. I mean, they'd force a store to take enough copies of the disk to sell for years.

But the funny thing was, of course, that it wouldn't take a store more than a week to unload and reorder. I mean, that platter was hot.

114

In no time we hit our millionth copy. They gave us the little old golden platter. And that disk just kept on selling.

So, naturally, we became the experts on everything.

If there's one thing I never have dug, it's the expert bit. Because a man writes a hit or a group has a hit disk, does that make them experts on everything?

Like, this one chick from a fan magazine came on real strong. "Stacy-baby," she started off, "what can you tell your fans, our readers, about the whole LSD scene? Do you make it big in the trip department?"

I shrugged. "That's not my scene, lady."

"Man," she said, "you don't want the kids to think you don't swing. Lay words on me about, uh, the atom bomb."

"It kills people," I said.

"Do you think we should disarm?" she asks.

I give her one of those when-did-your-saucer-land-on-Earth? looks. "Lady," I said, "I'm a piano player. What would I know about A-bombs?"

To this day I guess those reporters and writers haven't dug that I was putting them on. What is with this expert bit? What ever made me an expert? All the money we made off those two songs?

Is that the bit? Money makes you an expert? If you haven't got it, nobody cares what you think about anything. But if you're loaded with bread, they want your opinion on skirt-hems, Red China, and religion. What's more, they print it.

And it wasn't just the magazines, either. Or the newspapers. I knew Stacy Nova and the Flesh-Colored Bandaid were hot. Whatever we did was news, I guess. Whatever we said sold newspapers.

But it was still a surprise to me to find out that people believed what they read about us in the papers and magazines. I mean, at parties, I would listen to some of these chicks rave on. I would wonder if they were in their right minds.

"I think you're terribly deep," this one kook told me at a party given us by a Hollywood producer.

"What's deep?" I asked.

"You see?" she asked right back. "That's what I mean."

Figure that one out. Or another time at a blast they threw us in England when we played the Palladium. Afterwards, at this party, one of these groovy English birds came up to me.

"I quite approve of your stand on disarmament," she said.

What she really said was "Aw quot apryoove of yaw stand awn disawmamunt."

I squinted my eyes. This is supposed to help you hear better, right? I said: "My stand on what?"

"Absolutely," she said, nodding her head very hard.

Or another time backstage at the Ed Sullivan show. We were booked for two spots, closing the

116

first and the second half-hours. I had a bad ping in my piano amplifier during the first set. So at the break I took the back off the thing and started tracing the trouble.

"Want an electrician?" one of the production girls asked me.

"It's all right," I told her. "The trouble is either a loose connection or a potentiometer winding."

"Stop putting me on," she said, real smart.

I found the loose connection and crimped it closed with a pair of pliers. "That should do it," I said. It did.

After the show the production girl brought Ed Sullivan around for a private talk. "This boy is amazing," she gushed. "He's a real renaissance man."

"A what?" I asked.

I never did look it up, but I guess it was meant to be nice.

What with being booked in most of the big cities and recording the title song for a movie sound track and hitting all the big TV shows, I wasn't seeing too much of Carol.

As a matter of fact, about the time our big LP album was coming out, she called me. I was busy with one of the sound engineers when the phone rang. Normally I would have asked whoever it was calling to phone back later. But, seeing that it was Carol, I answered.

117

"I'm sorry to bother you," she began. "But I'm leaving for Ottumwa in an hour and I thought you ought to know."

There was a long kind of pause. I mean, what do you tell a chick who's walking out on you, especially when you're not at all that cracked up about her leaving?

"I'm sorry to hear that," I said. "How come you're going?"

It was her turn to take a long pause. "I'm sorry," she said then. "What did you say?"

"I'm sorry I mumbled. I asked you why you were leaving."

This time neither one of us broke the silence for a while. Finally, she said: "Oh, my mother's not feeling well. You know."

It wasn't the fact of her leaving that got me. All of a sudden it was the fact that she had dreamed up such a phony excuse. That really got me shook up. I mean, I meant so little to her that she didn't even bother cooking up an alibi that I could believe.

"I'm sorry to hear that," I said.

We seemed to have been telling each other nothing but "I'm sorry" for most of the conversation. Behind me the sound engineer was starting to get impatient. That got me angry, too.

If my girl was walking out on me with hardly a ghost of an excuse, who was he to get impatient? Or was she my girl any more?

118

"Listen," I began on the phone again, "you'll be back in town soon, won't you?"

"Back in New York?" Carol asked. "Why?"

"Come on."

"I mean it," she said. "Why? You and the boys aren't here that often, are you? And without you, I hate this place."

"And with me?" I asked. It was one of those cracks you're always sorry you shot off. If you get a lie for an answer, you know it's a lie. And if you get the truth, man, that's even worse.

"With you," Carol said, her voice getting a little hoarse, "it's like living in hell."

She hung up the phone so softly at her end that, at first I didn't even know we were cut off. I sent the sound engineer home, or wherever sound engineers go when they aren't engineering. It was a bad time for a while.

But the album was selling. Not as fast as the single 45 disk, but well enough. None of the songs in the album took off as singles, but we expected as much.

Colonel Crumpacker told me what we were earning. I could hardly believe how much it was, even after we cut it into pieces for each of us. Eddie and I got more than the others, of course, because we were the composers as well as performers.

"I've got to invest this money, boys," the Colonel would tell us.

But we had no idea how to do that. People came

119

around with all kinds of ideas. You know: stock that was sure to double our money, or a scheme to set up a gambling ship off the Florida coast. We nixed it all.

Eddie's father said we should invest in land. We bought lots of lots. I mean if there was any empty land around New York or Los Angeles or Chicago or Nashville, we bought it. We picked those towns because at least we got there once in a while.

We also set up our own music publishing company. We started promoting other people's songs. Some of them did all right, too.

Then Eddie and I went into the endorsement business. You dig that bit? Eddie let them put out ads for certain guitars or amplifiers. "I dig this brand the most," says Eddie Getz of the Flesh-Colored Bandaid. And collects a few thousand for it.

Colonel Crumpacker started getting us all kinds of endorsements. In one month I said I liked a pimple cream, a mouthwash, a toothpaste, a breakfast food and, of course, a certain kind of bandaid.

"It's too darned bad you boys ain't twenty-one years old yet," the Colonel complained. "I could get you lots of loot for endorsing brands of cigarettes and booze."

Don't ask me if I thought any of this stuff was good. At that point we were hot. The money was rolling in. There was very little we wouldn't do to keep it rolling in fast.

But there are so many ways to make money when

you're hot. I can't even remember all of them. Song pluggers would give us anything to cut a disk of a new number or sing it on a TV show.

I got a letter from Frankie in Chicago. "Dear Celebrity," she wrote. "Glad to see you are copping all the goodies. It's the American way, baby. Don't quit till they make you." Whatever that meant.

I got a letter from Yvonne. I got a letter from a chick I had seen a few times in Nashville. I got a letter from my old high school music teacher. I got a letter from my Aunt Tessie, the one who'd loaned my folks the piano. Naturally, my folks didn't write.

Neither did Carol.

I can remember all those things now. But at the time, I hardly even had time to read anything, let alone letters. The fan mail came in every day by the thousands. Three girls answered all the letters except the ones that were from old friends.

But when you're hot, you don't even have time to read letters from old friends. You only have time to read contracts and scripts. You only talk to agents and producers. You move fast because you're hot. And you're hot because you move fast.

I remember all kinds of famous people we met in those months. Mayors of cities and movie stars and astronauts and ballet dancers and generals and senators and prizefighters.

It got to be a kind of game for Eddie and me. The game was "Who's The Big Name Tonight?" And tonight there was always a party or a reception or a ball or something.

We'd either be guests or we'd be asked to perform. And there was always a Big Name. Besides Stacy Nova and the Flesh-Colored Bandaid, of course.

Eddie used to embarrass me. He had a little autograph book in his guitar case. He would whip it out and get autographs from everybody who was anybody.

"It doesn't look right," I'd say. "They should be asking for your autograph, not the other way around."

"You gotta be kidding," Eddie would say. "These are big names, Stosh."

"We have a big name, too."

"Yeah, but these cats have been big for a long time. Who knows about how long we'll last?"

Whenever he said something like that I could have taken a poke at him. I mean, when you're hot, you shouldn't even think of that kind of stuff.

Or so I thought.

28

You know, when you're a winner, you can't lose. I guess that sounds stupid. But it's a fact. You hit a winning streak and all doors open up.

Even so, a few things happen that make you wonder how much fun it is to keep winning.

With all the great stuff going for us those months,
some odds and ends made me stop and think. Chicks,
for instance.

I mean, you know how I dig chicks. But once we
hit that winning streak, the fun went out of chicks
overnight.

You think I'm putting you on? Me, complaining
because chicks were too easy to get?

That was the trouble. In the old days, back in
school or when I was gigging around Chicago, I made
out great. I knew a secret a lot of the guys didn't know.

Most guys in high schools are just starting to dig
chicks. And, of course, chicks always cool it. The secret is, no matter how they cool it, they dig guys as
much as guys dig them.

So, let's say I would have eyes for some new chick.
I knew that unless I did something really disgusting,
chances were she'd sort of have eyes for me. Maybe.
And that was the fun, the maybe.

Once Stacy Nova and the Flesh-Colored Bandaid
hit the big time, all that changed. We used to get
thousands of letters from chicks. They all wanted to
swing with us.

And, I mean these chicks didn't waste any time
beating around the bush. They just out and out laid
it on the line.

The ones who couldn't wait for answers to letters

used to wait for us outside the theatre at night. Sometimes we'd come off the stage, soaking wet from playing a big set, and find a few chicks stashed away in the dressing room.

We'd find them outside our hotel. We'd find them in the lobby. One night I hit the sack around two A.M. and a chick crawled out from under the bed.

Sounds like fun? Forget it.

A few other things were strictly for forgetting, too. About one out of every ten letters we got was a crank note.

I hope you don't get mail like that, ever. It comes from sick people with sick minds. It's got the kind of ideas and language in it that makes you sick just to read.

Of course, one letter I got did my heart good.

"Stacy-sweetheart," the letter began. It was typed on business paper with the name and address of the place printed on top. "How glad I am to see how big you're making it, baby. We always knew you had great stuff. Maybe you and I didn't always see eye to eye. But that's all past and forgotten.

"Any time you're in town, baby," the letter went on, "just drop by the old place. Everything's on the house. Everything's free, Stacy, because we love you, sweetheart."

It was signed with a guy's name. The printed heading on the letter? You guessed it: "Alky Lane."

That's right. The note was from Muscles, telling me

all was forgiven. Now, I ask you. How much can a guy crawl?

If he hated me enough to track me to Nashville that time, why didn't he still hate me? Answer: I was a big man now. Mob or no mob, Muscles wanted to patch it up.

It did my heart good. But I made a note never to show up in Alky Lane. Maybe he loved me now. But I still hated him.

Muscles' letter was nothing compared to the letters from people who wanted to sell me something. Insurance? Inventions? Song? Dating Service? Cemetery Plots? Cars? Apartments? Restaurants? Golf Courses? Night Clubs? Clothes? Boats? Apple Orchards? Fur Coats? Airplanes? Trips? You name it, somebody was peddling it.

The only thing nobody was trying to sell me was good advice. And that was the one thing I needed most.

29

I would say we hit the peak about the time we hit Chicago. You remember me telling you about it. Where I put on that news chick from the *Sun-Times*?

The big scene in the hotel suite with the manicurist and the champagne?

That was our high point. Of course, nobody knew it at the time. After that we did our movie. That was a gas and a half. They wanted us to do a kooky-type flick like the ones the Beatles do. At least, when we started on our tour, we were supposed to end up in Hollywood and do this kooky-type movie.

But by the time we got there, a month after our big Chicago scene, the whole movie had changed. Instead of a barrel of laughs, something new and different, it was another of those bikini-and-biceps movies. And we didn't exactly star in it.

We were "featured." That means we did a few numbers for the cameras. Later on these scenes were put into the movie at various places. Like the hero would be seen sitting on his beach blanket and he'd say:

"Let's go dig some groovy new sounds, baby."

And the whole sandy bunch of them would clomp off to the nearest auditorium or whatever and we'd do our number.

I think if I had been thinking about anything at all, I would have known we were past our peak. I mean, if you're really hot, they don't bury you in another beach epic.

Then, too, the sales on our album were dropping. Once the album came out, the 45 rpm. disk stopped selling much. We didn't care because we made a lot more on every album. But pretty soon the album re-orders slowed to a crawl.

I had a little heart-to-heart with Colonel Crumpacker.

"It's nothing, son," he assured me. "Everything has a beginning, a middle and an end. Your first album has run its course. Now it's time to blast the public wide open with the brilliant new number."

That made sense. Eddie and I worked like beavers. We rented a little shack in Malibu. That's a beach town on the coast near Los Angeles. We did nothing for three weeks but write songs and dunk in the surf.

I thought the numbers we wrote were pretty good.

"I think they stink," Eddie said.

"You thought 'Dead Abe' stank," I reminded him.

"Yeah, and you hated 'King of Things,' remember?" He frowned. "But those old numbers had something. Not one of these eight new songs has anything."

I shook my head. "Eddie, a song is just a song. Once we trick them up with groovy playing, the people will die for them."

Eddie looked even gloomier. His brown eyes had gotten very black and I thought he might be angry. "I think we're losing our touch," he said then. "Why should anybody pay money to hear these numbers?"

"Why did they pay to hear our first ones?"

"That's the point," Eddie said. "I didn't like 'Dead Abe' but it had something crazy, something goofy that got under people's skin. Since then there've been twelve imitations of it by other groups. Take 'King of Things.' It had something to say. People wanted to hear it. But so many other songs since then are like 'King of Things.' It's old hat."

"I'm with you," I agreed. "So what?"

"These eight new numbers of ours. They're imitations, too."

Now it was me getting angry. "That's a lie!" I snapped. "Stacy Nova and the Flesh-Colored Bandaid don't imitate. Other cats do our bag. But what we do, we invent fresh every time."

"Baloney," Eddie said. Actually he said a different word, a shorter one.

I'd heard it a lot from other people. But when Eddie said it, it hit me like a shot in the head. I jumped up from the chair. Outside the window, the Pacific Ocean was banging away at the shore. These terrific high combers were curling in like express trains and crashing down like bombs.

"Are you trying to tell me we're copying other people?" I asked. My voice was so high and so loud you could have said I was shouting.

"I'm not trying. I'm telling."

"You're a liar," I yelled.

I turned away from the window in time to see him pull on a pair of sneakers and walk out the front door.

"Eddie?" I called.

But he didn't turn back.

30

We had very little to say to each other after that day. I closed up the Malibu place. We rehearsed the new numbers.

Then we cut our tapes and got them sounding just right. The demos went out to the disk jockeys. The publicity stuff started to grind.

Bandaids Blast New Bag!

Stacy In-nova-ates Groovy New Sounds!

Get The Hottest Album in Disk History!

I had great hopes for one of the new numbers. I called it "Planet Number Three." It had these kind of wild, far-out harmonies, like "Dead Abe," only it had words.

The idea of "Planet Number Three" was that these Martian cats were watching it blow up. They didn't know the name of it. But it was the third planet from the sun.

Of course, the message was that the people on this planet couldn't agree on anything. So they had a big war. They blew up their whole planet. And the snapper was that the third planet from the sun is Earth. Dig?

Right. But nobody else seemed to.

The album was called "Visitors From Planet Three." The cover had one of these psyched-out freak color photos of the Bandaid and it was a real groove.

I would check all the disk shops in Los Angeles. We moved east and did gigs in Des Moines, St. Louis, Cleveland and Miami. I checked the shops in all the towns.

They all featured the album. I mean, our record company had good salesmen. The album was always in the window. Cartons of it were opened up and stacked around the stores.

But nobody was coming in to buy them.

I asked Colonel Crumpacker what was the beef. "Son, there is a time and a place for everything. This is not the time for the Planet Three album I guess."

"And Earth isn't the place for us," I finished. "What do we do, Colonel-baby?"

He shrugged. "We sit tight and hope for the best."

Well, I did more than that. I promoted that album on every radio and TV talk show you ever heard of. I would travel anywhere to talk. I hit Minneapolis and Spokane and Missoula and Phoenix and Baton Rouge and Atlanta and Pittsburgh and Detroit and you name the town, I was on the air yacking up a storm about the album.

And in the shops, the album lay there like a corpse.

It was dead, all right, and so were we. But nobody knew it yet.

I talked to Eddie about it, but he wasn't saying any more to me than "hello" and "pass the salt." I got a letter from Carol postmarked a month before. It had taken that long for the fan-mail girls to weed it out and forward it to me. Not that they had that much fan mail to check any more.

"Dear Stacy," she wrote. "I miss you so much. In the magazines, they say you and the boys are having trouble. But it's all lies, isn't it? You were always so full of confidence and talent. I know—"

Here she had crossed out something so I couldn't read it. "Mom is feeling much better," she went on. "It's very peaceful here. I think of you traveling on the road and I ache for you. It's no life, is it?"

I nodded, reading it, as if she had actually said it to my face, instead of in a month-old letter. "Maybe you'll find a peaceful place of your own some day," she wrote. "Everybody needs a place like that. When I hear you on the radio, you sound rushed. You sound all churned up. Please, Stacy, please stop for a while now and then."

I phoned her immediately. "Can you leave Ottumwa, baby?" I asked her.

"For where?" she wanted to know.

The connection wasn't so hot. We couldn't hear each other too well. I told her I missed her. I said her letter made me feel funny. I asked her to come east for a visit.

"For what?" she wanted to know.

I gave up after a while. I mean, I couldn't tell her what was really bugging me. So I was sort of lying all the time to her. Anyway, what could she have done to help?

The Colonel was no help, either. He talked about "jacking up the sales effort." He wanted to book me on more talk shows for radio. He wanted the record company to spend more on advertising.

But the plain fact was that few people liked the new album. Very few bought it. I mean, say what you want, the truth of it was plain.

So I went to Eddie and apologized.

"I was wrong," I said. "I guess the album is a bunch of warmed-over steals from other people. I guess that's why nobody likes it very much."

He gave me a long look. "I guess so," he said. Then: "What next?"

I blinked. "For us?"

He nodded. "Do we want to keep playing these one-night gigs? Till they stop booking us because who ever heard of us?"

"The public isn't that fickle."

He thought about this for a while. "Maybe not. A few groups keep making it big year after year. But they change. They experiment. They do new things. They don't copy. They invent."

My cheeks felt as if they were burning. "I dig."

"You should," Eddie said. "Because you're the one who really writes these numbers. I work up the

132

chords and changes, but the idea is always yours. And, Stosh, the ideas are what counts."

"I dig."

"So, what's next?"

"I don't want to keep working till they stop wanting to hear us," I said. "If I'm going to drop out of sight, let it be me who calls the drop. Fast. Before people know what's happened."

"They know already," Eddie said. "The kids who buy records are hip to what's happened. They don't want to spend their money on stale stuff. You have to keep yourself new or these kids walk away from you."

"These kids?" I had to laugh. "I just turned twenty, Eddie. Does that make me an old man compared to them?"

"No." He sounded very serious and his eyes looked terribly dark. "No," he said, "you're not an old man. You're just a has-been."

I must have looked hurt. I didn't say anything, but my eyes must have showed how I felt.

"Don't let it bug you, Stosh," he said. "I'm a has-been, too."

I stood there, saying nothing, for a long time. "Well," I said then, "it looks as if the joke's on me after all."

"How so?"

"I guess for the last few months, when we were so hot, I was being just another King of Things."

"Sure."

"Just busy collecting things. Money things."

"Sure," Eddie agreed. "But don't let it bug you."

"I'm not bugged. I'm shocked at me."

"Just don't let it shock you too far off base."

I frowned at him. "Meaning what?"

"Meaning, you have to try to find out what it was that you did right. Then you have to try to do it right again."

"It was luck the first time," I said. "I always knew it was luck. This proves it."

"You have to have luck. But that's only part of it."

I sat down in Eddie's hotel room. We were playing a two-night gig in Youngstown, Ohio. We had another night to go.

I thought about how I had been at first. How sure I had been. How the songs had come so easily. How the big break came. Everything.

I decided success was like pot. It could distract you. It could keep you from knowing what was really happening to you.

All the time I was hot and the money was pouring in, I wasn't learning anything. I was standing still. Nothing new was hitting my brain. It was as if success put a thick glass cage around me.

Now the glass was gone. I could hear the world again. I knew what was happening.

And I didn't like it.

31

Once when I was about fifteen, I was fooling around with an electric piano that belonged to somebody else.

I opened up the back to see what made it work. I think maybe I was using a pocket knife for a screwdriver. Anyway, the tip of the knife hit one of the power transformers. The spark jumped a foot.

The next thing I knew I was halfway across the room on my back.

I hopped up on my feet like a jack-in-the-box. I started running.

I ran out the door, down the hall and out the front door. I ran along the sidewalk. I ran about three blocks. Then I turned a corner and ran some more.

I think maybe I ran for about fifteen minutes. When I stopped I was out of breath. I just flopped down on somebody's grass lawn. I lay there gasping for breath. It took me another fifteen minutes till I was breathing right.

Then I walked home.

That's what an electric shock did to me once. I hear shock affects different people in different ways.

Some people freeze up. Some start running. Now you know which kind I am.

So I cancelled our second night in Youngstown. "Eddie," I said, "I'm taking off."

"What?" I could see he didn't believe me.

"The Flesh-Colored Bandaid will have to make it without Stacy Nova," I told him.

"You have to be kidding. What kind of act is it without you?"

I shrugged. "Maybe good enough to get along. Maybe not. Why don't you find out?"

I didn't stand around waiting to hear any arguments. I left Eddie standing there in his hotel room. I packed and got to the airport fast.

The first flight to anywhere was a little puddle-jumper going to St. Louis. I took it. I remember once in England at some party, I got to talking with one of the Beatles. I can't remember which one. I was telling him about taking the first train out of Nashville that time.

"It's kind of like flipping a coin," I said. "You take the first train or plane and see what happens."

Of course, once you get a shock and start running, all that happens is you keep on running. I hit St. Louis at midnight and, baby, there was nothing going out of that Lambert Airport till morning.

So I went to the train depot. A train that had started out in life in Louisville, Kentucky, was slowly

136

pulling into the station. I got my bags on board and fell asleep in one of the coach seats.

About two A.M. the conductor came through.

"Where'd you get on, young fella?" he asked me. In the dark I must not have filled him with too much ease. I wasn't wearing the electric turban, but I had on one of these groovy deerstalker caps. You know, the Sherlock Holmes jobs with the front-and-back beaks.

"St. Louis," I admitted.

"Where you getting off?" he asked, pulling out his ticket-making thingie.

I thought for a while. "Uh, what towns have you got?"

"Well, we got—" He stopped and stared at me. "Don't you know where you're going?"

"Of course," I said. "But just refresh my memory."

"We got Kansas City, Omaha, Sioux City, Sioux Falls—"

"Give me Omaha," I cut in.

When we reached Omaha the sun was out. It was morning. I needed a shave and a shower and a change of clothes. I needed a night's sleep in a bed. But the shock hadn't worn off.

I stood around in the train station wondering what to do. I could still feel the tingling from the shock. I had to keep running.

I walked a few blocks to the bus depot. I mean,

after all, I'd tried plane and train without too much luck. The next bus was headed for Chicago.

I took it.

You don't believe in fate, do you? I mean, the next bus out was heading to my home. Is that fate or is that fate?

But if you believe in fate, baby, you better be ready for some awful kinky twists.

Like the first stop was a major city named Atlantic, Iowa. The second was a giant town name of Des Moines. The third city the bus pulled into was the charming village of Oskaloosa, Iowa.

And the fourth town was Ottumwa.

32

I was reading one of the fan magazines the other day. I haven't read one in about six months. The magazine had an interview with Eddie Getz.

"Do you and the Bandaid still miss Stacy Nova?" he was asked.

"Do we ever," Eddie said. "If he came back tomorrow I'd be the happiest man in the whole music business."

"Still and all," the interviewer asked, "the Bandaid is doing rather well as a trio. Your new record has sold half a million copies."

"It's not the same without old Stosh," Eddie said.

"By the way, where is Nova?"

"He wouldn't want me to tell you," Eddie said.

"Is he in hiding?"

"Nothing like that," Eddie told the interviewer. "He may be back in the music world any day now. Or he might decide not to return at all."

The guy reading this in the fan magazine was my height, age and weight. But he had a short crew haircut and no moustache. He was wearing a white T-shirt and khaki chinos. He was lying on a big couch swing on the porch of this big old white-painted house on a side street in Ottumwa, Iowa.

His name was Stanley Novotny. That's the way it read on the marriage certificate. I thought my old lady would bust the day I phoned her long distance to invite her to the wedding.

They both came. My mother and Charley, the King of Things.

He said nothing to me at all at first. I introduced him to Carol's mother and father and her two brothers and her kid sister. He looked around the house. He may even have counted the rooms. If so, he found there were twelve rooms on three floors.

Then he cornered me in the garage. I was busy dusting off the car we were going to use on our honeymoon.

"That yours?" he asked after almost two years.

Not "Hello, son." Not even "Hello, you bum."

"Yeh," I said. Out in Iowa we don't waste too many syllables.

"Nice," he said.

This is a Jaguar XK-E painted the color of an unripe Mackintosh apple. It set me back six big skins and Charley says "nice."

He jerked his chin at the other car in the garage. It's a little Cougar I bought to go to the store in. "That yours, too?"

"Yeh."

"Umm." He stood around for a while. "That Carol is a very pretty girl. I guess," he said then, "the family has money."

I finished polishing most of the Jag's hood before I could trust myself to answer him. "Is that what you think?" I said then. "I married her for her money?"

Something about the tone of my voice made him keep quiet. "Or," I went on, "do you figure the only way I would ever lay hands on money was by marrying some?"

He frowned. "I didn't say that."

"You just thought it."

He thought about that thought. "No," he said then. "I figured you earned it." His voice sounded kind of tight, as if his throat pinched at the words.

"You mean I didn't come back to you begging for money?" I asked.

He frowned again. "You have a lousy memory. You remember too much."

We stared at each other. Then he smiled. I smiled. "Want to go for a ride in the Jag?" I said then.

"Too rich for my blood, son." He laughed slightly. "I'm not a rich man. Just the father of a rich man."

I put away the polishing cloth and we started back toward the house. "I'm not rich," I said. "I made money, all right, but it's mostly invested in land. The Colonel sends me a check every month, out of the money he's holding for me in the Nova Company."

He nodded. "You did pretty well, Stan," he said. "Or should I call you Stacy now?"

"Stacy is my stage name," I said. "I don't even know if I'd ever go back to show business. I'm starting to write a few new songs. But they're still bad. I lost whatever it was I had. It's not back yet."

We sat down on the back steps of Carol's house. I could smell the pork roast in the kitchen oven. In the garden, bees were buzzing around the flowers.

"What'd you lose?" he asked me.

"The knack of writing songs people like."

He shrugged. "You'll get it back."

"You have to believe what you're writing." I turned to look at him. "At this point, there isn't anything I'd want to write a song about."

"Not even something like King of Things?" he asked me.

He wouldn't look at me. He was watching the bees in the garden. "I didn't know you'd ever heard that number," I said.

He nodded. "You sure believed in that one," he said then.

Still he wouldn't look at me. "Did you like it?" I asked.

"Oh, sure," he said sarcastically.

"I mean—"

"Forget it," he cut in. "It was a pretty good song, Stan. It had a pretty good idea."

Carol came to the back door. "We've been looking all over for you two," she said.

"We're coming," my father said. He stood up. "Stan and I haven't talked in some time."

"Yeah," I said. "Listen. Call me Stosh."

Leslie Waller's two teen-age daughters are responsible for their father being "hooked on rock." And once "hooked," Mr. Waller spent months listening to many, many groups and talking to their individual members, before he began writing this convincing picture of the contemporary music scene.

His experience as a reporter and free-lance writer (he is the author of several novels and nonfiction books) helped him immeasurably. So did his experience playing in a band when he was in high school and college. Mr. Waller lives in New York City, is a graduate of the University of Chicago and holds a master's degree from Columbia University.

Juv
WI98n